Maxim Jakubowski

was born in Barnet but brought up in Paris. He followed a career in publishing by opening the Murder One bookshop in London in 1988. He writes, edits and publishes in many areas of genre fiction, including SF and fantasy, mystery and erotica. He edited the best-selling *Mammoth Book of Erotica* and its follow-up, *The Mammoth Book of International Erotica*. As publisher, he has been responsible for various cult imprints, including *Black Box Thrillers*, *Blue Murder* and *Eros Plus*. He has also published over thirty books of his own, including *The Great Movies Live*, *London Noir*, the *New Crimes* series, *Royal Crimes*, *Murders For The Fireside* and *No Alibi*.

He is an official advisor to several international film festivals, writes for a variety of publications, including *The Observer*, *The Big Issue*, and *The Guardian*, and reviews crime in a monthly column in *Time Out*. He is also contributing editor to *Mystery Scene* and a winner of the Anthony Award.

In his spare time he dreams of the beauty of women and hopes one day to complete his *Encyclopedia of Hard-Boiled Fiction* and a novel — which will, of course, feature women, guns and blood.

This collection first Published in Great Britain in 1996 by
The Do-Not Press
PO Box 4215
London SE23 2QD

A Paperback Original

Collection copyright © 1996 by Maxim Jakubowski
All rights reserved

ISBN 1 899344 06 3

British Library Cataloguing in Publication Data. A catalogue record for
this book is available from the British Library.

Printed and bound in Great Britain by The Guernsey Press Co Ltd,
Guernsey, Channel Islands

Life In The World Of Women

a collection of vile, dangerous and loving stories by

Maxim Jakubowski

THE DO-NOT PRESS

Contents

Here my dear, this landscape after the battle.

'Here she is then, all her guises under one cover.'
(Ellen Gilchrist)

The KC Suite

My original sin was to need you who could live without me... I re-
sisted as best I could, not knowing that the struggles of the soul are in-
tended to be lost.

Marie-Victoire Rouillier

I sing the sacred. I sing the bodies, I sing the sex, the union between man and woman, the ever so shocking intimacy of bodies moving towards each other, of copulation, of fornication,
on beds of starched linen sheets, on floors of unclean carpet
squares, on rickety sofas, in bath tubs under the drip of a leaking
shower head, in adulterous beds where the smell of deceived
partners still lingers on, in public places, in private places. I sing
the fucking, the thrusting, the sighs, the pain and the pleasure.

I sing what is no longer. I mourn what we once were and if you
say I am betraying you thus, I say you are wrong. It might be a
wake, but it is also a celebration. Of the way our naked flesh met
and connected and of a joy supreme.

This is what happened.

This is a crime story I wrote and published somewhere. At one
stage I thought it might actually become the opening chapter for
a novel I was mentally toying with, about violence and desire
along the American highways and a desperate race for love and
money moving from Florida to Seattle. I read it in public at some
festival. She was in the audience. As I hesitantly lingered over
the particularly sexual elements, aware that my tale was so much
more personal and explicit than the preceding stories by my fel-

low authors, my eyes suddenly connected with hers. She was sitting in a middle row. For weeks afterwards, I would wrack my brain to try and recall the actual colour of her eyes, with no success. I would find out later, of course. I was sitting with three others on a slightly elevated platform, two microphones shared between the four of us, a carafe of water and glasses, green baize covering the table on which our books were scattered. I wonder what I must have looked like to her. I was wearing a black Wranglers shirt with metallic poppers, open at the collar, and my usual black Farah trousers. That shirt is still a favourite of mine, I enjoy the way the cuffs sport three poppers instead of the traditional lone button most shirts have. I don't remember what she wore. At the end of the reading, one or two people came over with questions. I lost sight of her as the audience trouped out of the large room.

This is the story I read that day. It was raining outside, pouring down with rage. The woman in the story was a composite of so many I had known and, in fact, was even more a creature of my imagination. When I wrote the tale, I had not yet visited Miami.

Rite of Seduction

'Kill me,' she had asked.

So I had.

It seemed the only thing to do. I can't pretend I was confused, I wasn't. I knew exactly what I was doing. I remember the night still: there was a full moon over Miami Beach, the ocean lapped the shore quietly and the cheap motel sported some odd Spanish name that somehow reminded me of a bad Elvis Presley song. It was fast, reasonably painless. The look in her eyes. Then she died.

She was a $100 a night starlet in a $2.5 million B-movie. I'd been hanging round the studios for a week or so. I had an assignment to cover the making of a big project financed by Spielberg's Amblin company for one of his young hot-shot screenwriter-turned-directors. My interviews were in the can, my notepad full of okay anecdotes and I was ready for the road home and a first draft on the laptop. That evening, I'd walked into this small projection room towards the back of the studio lot. Some indie outfit was screening its dailies. The assistant director had shared reviewing chores with me on a now defunct magazine some years back, and hearing I was schmoozing around town had suggested we have a drink together for old time's sake after the screening.

It was hot and sticky in the projection room. The conditioning had a bad case of terminal cough and it smelled inside there of dry sweat, stale cigarettes and dime store perfume.

On the screen, following disjointed shots that a clever editor would later knit into the semblance of a car chase with explosions and bruised metal galore, came take after take of a nude shower scene and graphic enactment of a rape. Shot with three different cameras, one hand-held, the sequence repeated and repeated punctuated by clapperboards snapping, seen from various angles, at times literally pornographic as the camera lingered on details of the girl's body, the ambiguous smile on her lips as some Latin American-looking hood first slapped her before throwing her onto the bed, her breast tips stiffening as both naked bodies made contact, a fleeting view of her slightly open pubes as the hand-held camera moved to a better vantage position, a candid shot which would no doubt land on the proverbial cutting-room floor. It was all badly filmed, but these soundless, imperfect images had an unsettling effect on me. In the smoky darkness, I could feel the dryness in my throat and the beginning of an involuntary erection.

For the other spectators in the uncomfortable room, it was nothing new or anything wild, just a strip of unformed celluloid that would fit into a larger visual puzzle once it had been cleaned up, aseptised. Most of them would have been present at the shooting anyway and this was just a bunch of flickering second-hand thrills.

The screen went dark as the projectionist threaded some new footage into the system. A bar scene with different protagonists I'd never seen before. The knot in my throat was beginning to hurt. I just had to get out of this room, hankered for a cold drink.

'I need some fresh air,' I whispered to my pal sitting in the next row. 'I'll see you outside later.'

As I rose from my seat, I noticed a woman in the back row of the small audience also heading for the exit.

Once in the open air, the cold was like a slap in the face following the suffocating atmosphere of the screening room. The woman who had preceded me out was standing with her back against the building's wall, a long filterless cigarette hanging from her lips.

'Do you have a light?'

It didn't take me long to recognise her. Clothing was no disguise. It was that ambiguous smile, part come-hither invitation, part crooked rictus, half small girl ingenue and half downtown hooker.

'Sorry, I don't smoke. But I badly need a drink of some sorts. There's a bar around the block, you can light up there.'

She appeared so much smaller than on the screen, but this was not unfamiliar. I introduced myself. Even minor film journalists might prove useful to a career girl, she must have initially thought, and followed me across the lot.

The bar was called something like The Mark of God in Spanish, or some other patently stupid or irrelevant name. It just sticks in my memory somehow. The lighting inside was gentle and soothing. I had my customary cola, no ice; she had a vodka and orange.

'Quite a sequence, hey?'

'Yeah.'

'It must feel odd,' I said, 'to see yourself up there so big, so… so…'

'Nude, you mean, naked?'

'Yes, I suppose that's what I was trying to say,' I answered.

She smiled gently. I wasn't blushing, but neither did I feel altogether at ease. After all, I had already seen so much of her, her exposed flesh, her concealed self.

'How does it feel, to have to do a nude scene for the cameras?' I asked, slipping into journo mode, as she sipped her alcohol in the non-descript, almost empty bar.

'Well, you feel in a way violated, there are all these people around. In a way, it all becomes a bit impersonal, but you know what, it's also something of a turn-on. Gives you power over all these men. They can look but they sure can't touch.'

'Really?'

'Oh yeah.'

That first night, we returned to my hotel room.

As I undressed her in the full, bright light I finally witnessed the true colours of her body. Seeing her on a cinema screen being touched by another man was one thing, and was quite enough to give me a hard on, but here, smaller, open to nobody but me, she was something else. Her skin felt softer than the skin of any woman I had been with before. For all that, she was hard and firm, her breasts pointing gently upwards, stiffening as my fingers began to skim their tips, her buttocks clenched together as I lowered her onto the bed.

Inside her, it was like fire, all-consuming heat that reached so deep, so far. It wasn't like love, it was desperation and we merged like strangers, uncomprehending witnesses to the mad urges of our bodies.

On the second night we went to her room in another mediocre beach motel with would-be art nouveau trimmings and a crumbling balcony overlooking the ocean.

This time I undressed her slowly, mentally filming every square inch of her flesh for memory everlasting. The curve of her neck, the almost invisible dimple in her chin, the forgotten trace of a scar on her forehead hidden by a lock of stray hair, the mole at the top of her back, the way her pubic hair curled and curled. We never did say much. We didn't really have that much to say to each other when we were not in bed. We soon realised we were creatures of lust and little else mattered.

For I think an hour I kissed, caressed, gently bit, made studied foreplay with her until she could stand it no longer and screamed out:

'Enough, I want you inside me now,' as she wrapped her hand around my cock.

Then, 'It feels so big, I don't know how it's going to fit,' and guided me in.

On the third day, we rented a room for the night in a better class of hotel, up north on Collins Avenue, towards the Aventura Mall. At the other end of the room, facing the bed, was a large circular mirror. She insisted I take her from behind and watched attentively in the mirror, as I laboured in her rear, thrusting for her appreciation and my own pleasure and hers, fascinated by the look on her face as sweat dripped from her forehead over our private cinema screen.

It was simple fucking, it wasn't love by any means. But I couldn't escape, all of me just wanted more. I should have returned to the magazine and the city by now, but she was here for a further week, with one final sequence, a death scene to be shot, where the script dictated she meet her fate at the hands of some sordid Mexican pimp (I did say it was a B-movie, didn't I?).

'I'm so raw.'

'Me too, but it feels good.'

'Look at me down there, I'm all red.'

I kissed her open wound, savouring the strong taste and pungent smell of her insides.

'Your curls are too long,' jokingly.

'So trim me, shave me.

I did, and later that day when I made love to her for the first time in her utterly nude incarnation, she got so wet and excited that she lost all control and peed all over the sheets.

From that moment onwards, we both knew we were going too far but there was nothing to hold us back. The moments of desire when our energy returned and we could make love again were the only thing we could look forward to.

It was summer and I suppose we weren't that young any more. You know how sometimes you're doing something you shouldn't and you just can't help it, you're just a spectator watching yourself at play and wrong. Ah, summer... The sun comes out at last and women, girls, now unencumbered of their thick sweaters, long skirts, dresses and their heavy coats, move like a lightweight symphony in the streets outside, the shape of their bodies so sweetly visible like never before, and you want them all.

Summer and you think: this is wonderful, this is terrible. But the fear is there lurking deep inside, telling you it's the last time something this special is going to happen to me, and I want it to last forever, even if there is pain and heartbreak at the end of the road. Live now, pay later. Seize the bloody fucking day.

Summer and she's so much more than a fantasy, a pornographic centrefold dream. You hold her breasts in a vice, twist her nipples counter- clockwise until you think she will complain of pain, but she smiles and says nothing. You make love in the bath, and you slide in and out of her like in an ocean. You fantasise about making love in a public place. You eat in a fancy restaurant and she is deliberately wearing no underwear, and only your eyes, silent accomplices, know.

Summer never lasts forever.

'What's the matter?'

'It hurts like hell when I go to the bathroom. We've been making love too much, my cystitis is playing up.'

'I didn't know.'

'Yeah, a lot of us girls suffer from it, but it's been a long time, I must say. Don't worry, I've got some pills for it, There is a side-effect, though, you know,'

'What?'

'For a few days, whenever I go to the bathroom, I'll be pissing all blue…'

'What are you doing?'

'Just taking the belt from your pants.'

Afternoon, the sun is setting outside the window, the curtain drapes fluttering in the air, somewhere in the distance, I imagined, the Cuban coast. A tropical fantasy.

She is standing by the bed, threading the belt out of his beige slacks, her lips wet, her short, brownish hair tousled the way he loves it dearly. She is wearing a black bra, cut low, upholding her long, dark nipples. Mental photographs. They've already made love once today, both sniffing a capsule of amyl nitrate, their bodies bucking like wild horses when the chemical rush reaches their brain. Afterwards, she had washed her hair, and returned to the room with a white towel wrapped around her head, otherwise nude. He had been lying on the bed, resting, daydreaming, and he had looked at her moving nonchalantly through the room, his gaze fixed on her lower stomach, the lips of her shaven sex, pink and bruised like the petals of some exotic flower.

'Come here,' he had asked. 'Take me in your mouth.'

She now holds the belt in one hand, a red silk scarf taken from her bag in the other, picks up two stockings hanging on the door and comes towards him.

'Tie me up,' she asks him.

'Really?'

'Yeah, you've never tried that before, have you?'

'Can't say I have.'

'Well, there always has to be a first time. Tie me hard, tie me firm, both hands and feet.'

She couldn't move and moaned under the weight of my body as I forced myself into her brusquely without foreplay. Later, she tied me down also. Then she licked every part of my body, starting from my toes, sucking on them in a way I had never experienced before, sending shivers through the whole length of me. In time, not only my cock, but my balls in her mouth.

Tomorrow, they would be shooting her final scene in the

movie, where Ramon, the Mexican pimp (played by an elderly French utility actor), catches her red-handed concealing part of the take from the heist and knifes her in the stomach, leaving her to die in a pool of blood, in the back room of the cantina.

Then, she would be returning to California where her agent had managed another good-time girl small cameo in some other movie no doubt bound straight for the video shelves.

'Go to the fridge and get a cube of ice.'

'What for?'

'Squeeze it inside me, I want to feel what it's like.'

'There?'

'No, behind.'

And later she would do it to me, too.

We were on the road to nowhere, prisoners of our senses. She returned from the studio that day, wearing a thin white cotton tee-shirt through which her sharp nipples were clearly visible.

I felt a pang of jealousy that other men might have seen her breasts thus on the drive back from the shoot.

'Well, that's it. I'm now officially out of work,' she said.

'How did it go?' I asked.

'Well, he killed me cleanly. We only needed three takes.'

'How does it feel to be killed?' the journalist in me asked her.

'It turned me on. I almost wet myself.'

'You slut,' I said, jokingly.

'Yeah, well, that's what I am,' she answered, laughing. 'But now, listen, I want you to do absolutely everything I tell you to. It's important, this might be our last time together and I want you to remember it forever.'

'Yes, boss.'

I undressed her, her body was on fire, feverish, burning with emotional incandescence, she bit my lips to the blood as I pulled her head back by her hair. I tied her up, watched her crucified body spread-eagled over the bed. I prepared to undress. My short-sleeve shirt was sticking to my torso like an unwanted skin.

'Cover my eyes,' she begged, as I lowered my body over hers.

And as we made love, it was as if we were buried in a deep well of despair as we both knew all too well this must be the last time. There was nowhere else to go. Nothing more that we could do. We had tried everything, every position and most perversities and still we wanted more, but it just wasn't there. Is this all there was to love? Togetherness and future domesticity surely could not be the answer, felt rather ridiculous a concept in fact; anything further would only dull the immediacy, the passion, the desire, the lust.

As we came, almost together, I opened my eyes and saw a tear rolling down her cheek. 'What is it?' I asked her solicitously.

'You know very well what it is,' she answered calmly.

Yes, I knew.

It was then she asked:

'Kill me.'

The sweat was drying over our bare bodies. There was a full moon over Miami Beach.

So I did.

The sound of her neck breaking was muted and gentle.

Outside, it's now raining. In the distance, I can hear the jets hovering over Coral Gables on their way to landing at the International Airport, ferrying passengers to and from South America. It's been a few days already. I'm feeling hungry. I still haven't dressed and sometimes I disgust myself as unwanted erections manifest themselves when I gaze at her dead body, laid out like a cross over the grey bedsheets. Her crooked smile is now permanently carved into her face, her pubic hairs are shyly growing back and her fixed eyes keep on watching me.

I wonder what she is thinking now.

* * *

Yes, that's the story that started it all.

I came across her late in the evening at the bar of the hotel where all the delegates to the festival were staying. I'd ventured into town with a bunch of other writers, in a group of twenty or so, and we had ended up in a decent curry place. I'd somehow managed to get myself squeezed in between two local nincom-poop librarians, half the length of the table away from a small, flame-haired Murdoch Empire book editor I sort of fancied. Through the spicy meal, I kept on thinking of how our eyes had crossed paths at the reading. It was almost midnight when we all returned to base and the small bar was crowded. There she was, standing in distracted conversation with a couple of reviewers. I then realised who she was: a junior editor for some small pub-lishing outfit whose books you never actually saw in shops but who seemed to profitably stay in business mainly stocking library shelves with totally unpromoted novels and churning out badly designed cookery books, new age clap-trap and self-help and how to dress manuals.

She stood out like a beacon. All blonde, curly-haired, wonderfully tall five feet ten of her. I looked at her. My heart skipped a proverbial beat. I walked over.

'Hello.'

'How are you?'

My imagination immediately ran out of things to say to her in this artificially social context.

'I'd like to talk about things someday,' I clumsily blurted out and made my excuses, as she probably gave me a strange look while I moved away.

The next morning, the final hours of the festival, I spotted her on her own on a seat in the hotel's reception area reading a paperback crime and mystery novel by one of the previous day's main speakers. She looked up as I passed by, moving towards the bar where I had some business with an American film director. Half an hour later, I returned, she was still sitting there, a picture of vulnerable beauty, wearing a long loose black dress with small white polka dots. I moved towards her.

'Have you enjoyed the festival?' I asked her.

She looked up at me, smiled, the dress slid slightly down her left side, baring her pale left shoulder and revealing a thin black bra strap.

'How are you getting back to London? I have spare passenger space in my car if you're interested.' I enquired.

'I have a lift,' she replied.

Then someone called me away, and when I looked back in her direction, she was gone.

I thought of her a lot on the motorway back.

The Secrets of Her Anatomy

Dear KC,

You were probably wondering on Sunday morning what the hell I wished to talk to you about. Sorry I left you guessing. I just didn't know what to say and how to say it, I suppose. The propriety of making a gentle pass at a beautiful woman eludes me when she has witnessed me the day before reading 'dirty bits' aloud in public.

At any rate, I must confess I found you wondrously attractive and have thought about you a lot since the weekend.

I'd love to see you again, if only to talk or have a meal. Would you?

Until then, I remain,

Lustfully but respectfully yours,

Maxim J.

Dear Maxim,

I somehow guessed that you were not really interested in discussing the art of crime fiction with the likes of me.

Your letter made me smile. Yes, I'd love to meet up for a drink. Give me a call.

Yours,

KC.

Three weeks elapsed before they finally met. She had been on holiday to Ireland in the meantime. Searching for her roots, she joked over the telephone.

On that first evening, following a drink and a meal, he found out she was married, while they sat in the basement of a noisy Soho pub. All the wrong tunes were blaring out from the jukebox.

'So where do we go from here?' he wondered.

But when he drove her back to her train station, she gently put her hand on his while they waited in the queue to exit the China Town underground car park.

Everything was unsaid, but they could feel the mutual attraction simmering in the air like electricity. All they had done was partly exchange life stories and publishing gossip, but she said: 'We must meet again.'

'Yes,' he concurred.

On the occasion of their second meeting a week later, they quickly agreed after the first round of drinks that all Soho pubs were much too noisy in the evening, and they must find somewhere else to talk. He suggested his office. As a director of the company, he had a set of keys and knew no one else would likely be in at that time of evening. She readily accepted.

As he switched the lights on, she said:

'Don't, it's too bright,' and pulled out a metal candle holder with a large candle speared in its centre from a Habitat paper bag, which had been buried in her backpack full of manuscripts. 'I thought this might come in useful.'

He found a match. In the flickering of the candle, he looked in awe at her amazon figure. He'd never been with a woman this tall before, he thought. Her tousled hair was a mass of Medusa-like curls. Her eyes, he now saw, were dark brown. He moved towards her and kissed her. She responded.

The thin coat of scarlet lipstick melted under his tongue, tasting slightly sweet. She opened her mouth wider and allowed him to insert his exploratory tongue. A warm stream of air from her lungs raced inside him. She skipped a breath.

That evening, he kissed her deep and passionately, touched her knee, her thigh but no higher. She wore an open neck short sleeve white sweater and after delicately moving his roving fingers repeatedly over her face, her nose, her chin, his hand moved downwards to her soft shoulder. There was a light brown mole at the onset of her cleavage. He caressed it, and moved his hand further and cupped her small left breast. She looked deeply into his eyes, anxious, interrogating, hopeful, but kept on saying nothing. His fingers slipped behind the thin fabric of the shirt, inside her bra and kneaded her nipple, then as she still offered no resistance he delicately pulled the breast away from the flimsy texture of her black bra. Then, the other. A dark beauty spot peered at him close to the aureola of the right breast. She stood there, her breasts unceremoniously, wantonly on display, as he drank in this exquisite vision of her. The colour of her nipples was a discreet pink in the overall pallor of her torso.

Later:

'I have to catch the train home,' she said, her upper clothing in disarray, her cheeks flushed, some buttons of his shirt undone.

'Where did you tell him you were?'

'With one of my authors.'

'Stay longer, please. I want to make love with you,' he asked her in the office penumbra.

'Not today, we just haven't got the time. Next time.'

'Are you sure?'

'Yes.'

'I'll find it so difficult to wait. Every minute until I see you again, I shall doubt you, I will fear that in the cold light of day all tonight's fumblings will appear foolhardy and wrong to you and you will change your mind.'

'I won't,' she replied. But once they were walking along the night road to Charing Cross station, she moved faster and faster, in her characteristically manly and slightly gawky way, and she said little, almost as if embarrassed to be with him in public, swimming through the evening crowd.

The next day, he sent a single red rose to her office, bought from a flower stall in Covent Garden.

Two days later, he received a letter telling him he had been right, and that the reality of their circumstances had appeared to her all too clearly as they had been walking towards her train. She just couldn't, she wrote. She didn't wish to hurt her husband, she just felt she could not deceive her husband, and how anyway could they conduct an affair without it becoming sordid, cheap hotel assignments, stealing time out of time, deceitful. No, she just couldn't. He felt right gutted and answered as best he could, with a long letter justifying his feelings, the state his life was in and could not help himself evoking the erotic feelings she stirred inside him, how he already dreamed of their lovemaking, the caress of flesh against flesh, how their skin touching would feel. Please, he implored, change your mind. But he didn't really think she would and after receiving no answer, all he could do was write again. The hours and the days were heavy and lasted forever those weeks. Then another letter, and another. The tone moved from loving, suggestive, explicit to angry, resigned, desperate.

She phoned.

'Your last letter made me very angry (he could not for the sake of him recall what he had said in it that he he had not written before). But I just keep on thinking of you in spite of myself. We must meet again and talk.'

They settled for the bar of a big hotel.

He explained again, she nodded her understanding; he told her how he did not wish to harm anyone, that this was just between the two of them, that no one else would know, and as long as no one was hurt, why did they not accept what was happening between them and the way they felt?

Sipping her drink, she looked breathtakingly radiant. His heart was just ragged, being with her, detailing every facet of her features, the way her nose turned slightly upwards, her hair hid her ears, how the faint trace of a scar on her right cheek revealed itself in the bar's muted lighting.

She acquiesced in silence, her eyes piercing through him, her sadness touching him in parts he didn't know he had, her long dark stockinged leg like an endless object of desire parting her orange slit skirt.

He looked back at her, he hadn't even asked a question.

Their eyes, soundless.

'Yes,' she said, almost inaudibly, under her breath, and looked down at her lap.

'You mean?'

'Yes, I will,' she firmly answered.

He was overcome with naked fear rather than joy. She was saying she would become his lover, did she? Or was he interpreting her wrong?

'But we must agree we must not ever harm others, it's very important. You said so yourself.'

Immense relief coursed through him. And irrational disbelief. This can't be happening to me, surely?

'You won't change your mind again, will you?' he asked her, falling into fourth gear into a pit of newly-found insecurity.

'I promise I won't,' she assured him.

At last, he allowed himself to smile, to relax. The waiter brought some more peanuts and olives to their table.

'When?' he finally asked, after what he felt was a decent interval, after they had become more talkative and managed to cast the ghost of the coming affair aside to laugh a bit about publishing and writers' gossip. He loved the way she tittered when he said anything a touch witty or mischievous.

'I don't know. I hadn't thought about it, really.'

'I don't want the first time to be vulgar or sordid,' he said. 'Not at the office. I'll think of some hotel where no one knows us or is likely to recognise either of us. I'll make the arrangements.'

She nodded.

It would be two weeks. In the meantime, she came once more to his office a few nights later, and she allowed him to undress her when they embraced on the uncomfortable sofa he kept for visitors. But when he wanted to pull her black knickers down over her wide, ample hips, she said 'Not now, we must keep something for next time.' She had arranged a day away from her company, under pretext of some imaginary contracts seminar. He agreed, and touched her sex through the dark, thin material, she felt wet and so warm.

Cos I know that you
With your heart beating
And your eyes shining
Will be thinking of me
Lying with you on a Tuesday morning.

The Pogues

They became lovers on a Tuesday morning in August, in the identikit room of a chain hotel in the metaphorical shadow of the Heathrow runways. JG Ballard territory almost.

He had brought along a bottle of white wine and strawberries bought earlier that morning from a small greengrocer near Hampstead Pond, before picking her up in front of the tube station. She wore dark glasses during the drive.

'You're sure you still want to go through with this?'

'Of course I do.'

'I thought you might have changed your mind.'

'I thought you would.'

'Well, I was going to give you a few more minutes and then I was going to leave, thinking how can the bastard be late or not come?'

'I was here on time, but I was looking out for you in front of the cinema on the other side of the road. I almost missed you …'

He undressed her first. Item by item. Layer by layer. Her waistcoat. Her long flowing skirt of many colours. Her quaint lace-up boots. Her wedding and engagement rings. Kissed her throat, then her lips, then bit gently on her ear, nonchalantly licked her forehead and her smooth shoulders. Pressed his lips against her throat and held her tight against him. She wore a black bustier, garter belt and stockings.

'How lovely. It's been ages since I've seen stockings, old-fashioned but so nice, watching you like this is enough to turn anyone into a raving fetishist…'

'I thought you would like them.'

After rolling the warm silk down her endless legs and briefly tickling her funny-shaped toes, he got up from where he had been kneeling, drank in her sheer splendour and pulled down her final piece of underwear.

Her pubic hair was darker than he expected, all flattened curls against the marble expanse of her lower stomach. He kissed her bush with reverence, like a priest in holy homage.

He pulled back.

She was now nude.

The look in her eyes said a million things.

'I want to know everything about you,' he blurted out.

She turned round, took a few steps towards the window and closed the curtain.

'It's too bright,' she said.

It was only eleven-fifteen in the morning. The sun shone outside. All that could be seen from the hotel room window was a car park.

Her arse was slightly square and also heart-shaped, a tad too large, but he wanted his hands all over her pale cheeks. Venus on a Tuesday, he distractedly thought. The straps of the garter belt had left a small indent at the top of her hips, outlining the majesty of the pelvis where her dark cunt beckoned.

'Aren't you getting undressed?' she said.

He did, holding his stomach in as he pulled his trousers off. She looked him up and down.

He took her by the hand and pulled her towards the bed.

Later, when he would recall their first time together, the image of her body next to him with the filtered light that came through the curtains shadowing it delicately, would remind him of a postcard he had in his study of a sand dune, where a dip in the sand evoked a woman's navel and a rise the gentle slope of her small breast.

After the initial, obligatory nervousness, he surprised himself by managing erection after erection anew and making love repeatedly, entering her three times before the time came to clean up, leave the room rented for half a day and drive back to Charing Cross station for her six-fourteen train.

'Oh, God,' he says, entering her, feeling the ridged texture of her cunt walls against the taut skin of his cock.

'Oh, Jeeeeezus,' she says, as he slides, thrusts in and out of her, realising this is it, she has done it, she has a lover, she is an adulteress, and no longer fighting the pleasure coursing through her body.

'Oh, Christ,' he moans, his body convulsing as he comes inside her, and this is the first time, I want it to last forever, for eternity, and opens his eyes and notices she had kept hers open all along, the first woman he remembers making love to who has done so. What a wonderful quirk, he thinks. It strikes him deep. It touches him intensely.

Both speechless for a long time after the initial shared orgasm; he finally disengaged from her, pulling his now limp and moist penis from the warmth of her vagina and kissed her lips with all the tenderness he could muster, even as he knew that neither gestures nor words could properly express the epiphany he had just experienced. The cover of the bed is rumpled, they had not even bothered pulling it down to uncover the sheets. He gets up, pours her a glass of wine. His throat is dry.

'Shall we take a bath?' she asks.

Together in the regulation-size Trust House Forte bath tub which barely contains the two of them, he sees the dark bruises on her thighs and legs.

'Oh, it's nothing, I'm always catching the corner of my desk at the office. I bruise so easily.'

He soaps her, his fingers lingering more than hygiene demands in the gaping crack of her cunt, caresses her breasts with lather until they shine like wet jewels, she rubs his back, remarks on the hairy birth-mark there, he kisses her and their wet bodies entwine in the lukewarm water, he tries to manipulate himself into a position where he can enter her, but the geometry of the bath tub defeats him. He is hard. Dripping over the bathroom tiles and then the bedroom's grey carpet, they rush to the bed. Here, unbidden, she opens her mouth over his prone body and takes his penis into her mouth. He closes his eyes, thinking, Christ, and this is only our first time, and feels her teeth graze against his glans. He watches her tousled hair, the million and one blonde curls bob up and down over his stomach, observes the regal expanse of her back and her rising anus as she sucks with loving gluttony on his cock. He extends his hand and touches her back, a finger circling the black beauty spot just below her right buttock, the soft invisible golden down in the small of her back that reminds him of sheer silk in its tactile delight. He feels a surge pass through his body and pulls her off his member, lays her out on the white sheets, spreads her legs wide, slips a wet finger into the gaping aperture of her vagina and guides his cock in to the hilt. He feels harder, thicker and longer than he has ever been. He digs in as deep as he can, scraping, thrusting, aiming at her most intimate innards, she moans, her eyes open, gazing deep into him, her hair falling back from her face, revealing her over-large forehead, her exquisite innocence, her torn ear from a past accident with an earring that somehow got caught and was wrenched away, he pulls her legs up and places them over his shoulders, to increase the depth of his invasion, his hands move convulsively from her lips, to her shoulders, her breasts and move downwards to her arse. Impulsively, feeling the wetness in the valley separating her arse cheeks, he slips a finger into her anus. She screams with pleasure and comes instantly with a violent shuddering that courses in overdrive through her body from scalp to toes.

'Oh, Jeeeeezus, Jesus.'

They managed to get together again a week later. Initially, they were only going to see a movie. Some American indie effort. Throughout the film, he kept on wanting to touch her everywhere and found it difficult to concentrate on the pyrotechnic action on the screen.

'Me too,' she said to him as the credits rolled.

They rushed to his office, where they quickly stripped. Again she was wearing stockings and suspenders. He wondered, was it only for him? They fell on the hard floor and embraced, his cock straining for her in physical agony, his tongue inside her mouth, coming up for air when the pressure became too much. He kissed her everywhere, between her toes where she was ticklish, he licked her breasts, her stomach, counted every mole and mark on her body, imagining he knew every square inch of her flesh so much better than her husband did, he moved his tongue from cheek to cheek on her backside and slid it down the valley of her arse and into her rear hole. She shivered. Later, he slipped his finger in, and then two.

'You're so sensitive there,' he remarked.

'I know, I know,' she replied.

Later, in the days apart, he would dream of buggery. He knew she did.

He then moved her round onto her back and moved his mouth towards her sex.

'You can't,' she said. 'I have a tampon in. It's my period.'

Nonetheless, he slipped a finger into her sex and felt the moistness and the unbearable heat.

'Let me pull it out,' he asked her.

'Oh, you wouldn't,' she said.

And he began to tug gently on the thin string that peered out shyly from the folds of her labia, below the hood of her clitoris.

'I'll do it myself,' she said and stood up, all 5ft 10 of nude pallor and unforgettable flesh, and walked to the toilet in the corridor of the empty building.

When she returned, he entered her with joy. Later, when his cock slipped out of her, it was baked with blood, and when she moved over, there was a dark red stain on the brown sofa which he cleaned as best he could. To this day, there is a remote trace of it, and his heart stops every time he looks at the damn sofa, to the extent that he feels he should get rid of it as the memories assault him all too painfully.

There were many more encounters in his office over the months that followed. Often crazed coupling punctuated by doubt and guilt and snacks on the floor, sate sticks, prawns from Tesco, sushi pieces. Because both their backs ached every next day after lovemaking on the hard carpeted floor — they never did use the sofa again — he bought a thick orange blanket which they would drape over the floor, their bed of illicit sex, and later, when autumn came, he even acquired a cushion, and a quilted bed cover to keep them warm. He wondered what his secretary thought if she ever came cross the blanket, cushion and cover, at the bottom of his personal filing cabinet.

And then came the fateful weekend away in Brighton, after he had begged her repeatedly for a whole day, a whole night at least together for the first time. It had been her birthday the day before. Her husband had bought her a brown leather waistcoat and taken her to *Miss Saigon* in the evening. She had found the performance dreary and, somehow, nerves about the coming weekend, impatience with him or guilt, they had begun quarrelling and he had ended up sleeping apart from her on their small apartment's sofa bed.

The hotel was on the sea front. They took a cab from the station. Their alibi was another writers' conference. In the room, as he had previously promised he would when guessing randomly at her many secret fantasies, he borrowed the lipstick from her handbag, and pressed the soft tube against her breasts and rouged the nipples a dark red, then squeezed her body tight against his own, slashes of colour blending into the hair on his chest. Then he laid her out on the bed, set our her limbs in a semblance of crucifixion, held the fleshy folds of her cunt apart and applied the lipstick to its outer lips. Then, they fucked and he told her that he loved her, and he whispered suggestively to her what they would do throughout the coming night, how he would wake her and enter her in the small hours of morning, how he would remain embedded in her warm cunt while they briefly slept. Fingers, almost his whole hand, then his tongue in her various apertures, bringing her to climax again and again in moist abandon while he waited for his cock to grow hard between the successive bouts of lovemaking. Fish and chips on the promenade for lunch. Back to the room. Sex. Ice-cream at the local Haagen-Dazs parlour. Sex. Tying her hands against the foot of the bed with the belt he threaded out of his trousers, wrapping one of her black stockings around her neck as he took her from behind. A late night meal at a noisy Mexican joint a few yards from the hotel. The room, a small isolated world away from the real world. Washing her in the bath, joining her there, listening to her pee from behind the bathroom door, furtively sniffing her knickers. Shaving in the morning, naked, with his back to her while she relaxed in the tub, it all felt so familiar, so comfortable, so natural.

He had of course soon realised he was hopelessly in love with her. It wasn't just the sex, he knew. He just wanted to be with her all the time, holding her in his arms, buying her things, clothes, discovering books, music and movies together and he counted the interminable hours that would elapse between their stolen evenings and their furtive lunch hours in pubs none of their acquaintances frequented. He wanted more of her, all of her, and began pressuring her, which made her nervous. Her husband and her had sold their small, claustrophobic flat and had to find a new house to move into soon. Irrationally — even though he would eventually be proven right — he felt this new house would be the cause of the end of their relationship.

'Of course not,' she defended herself. 'We have to live somewhere, you know.'

On the Sunday morning, after breakfast, she rang her husband from the hotel lobby as she had agreed to and found out, to increasing panic, through talking to his brother when she could not reach him, that he had been trying to get hold of her the previous evening and had discovered she was neither registered at the conference nor resident at the hotel where the event was taking place. He had to drive up to Oxford unexpectedly and had only wanted to warn her. She burst out in tears when she returned to the room.

He clumsily attempted to comfort her, only for her to turn viciously against him. He was blamed for breaking up her marriage and she insisted they leave for London — immediately. It turned out to be a false alarm, and she lied her way through it, blaming matters on a mix-up between the hotel and the conference organisers. She said her husband was so immersed in his own job that he never even suspected. But the rot had set in. Having almost lost her, he now knew how much she really meant to him and he became absolutely terrified of losing her for good. He could no longer envisage life without her.

In his mind's eye, he no longer wanted her to be the wave, but the sea.

Autumn deepened.

She had to go to the Frankfurt Book Fair as all dutiful publishers do. He had a book to promote in America. From her bleak German room, she ached for him and wished he was there with her, she said. In his impersonal mid-West motel suite, he pined for her and feared she would no longer wish to see him after their return from foreign climes. She was due to move house a few days after Frankfurt.

They did meet up again a few times, and the sex was as intense as the pain they both felt about the future. Searing, savage, filthy, entering her again and feeling a desire to literally impale her, tear her apart from orifice to orifice. Shades of Bertolucci's *Last Tango*, he carried a small amount of butter in a plastic bag in his attache case, meaning to use it with her and penetrate her anally, but he never did, the tenderness of entering her conventionally sufficing in the gentle heat of the moment.

The fear and the uncertainty were driving him crazy. Should they part or should they stay together, where was it all leading to, did the others suspect, was the pain stronger than the joy the affair gave them? During a pub lunch break, she suggested they might stay apart for at least a month to consider their feelings and the situation. She was now thinking of him too much, she said, in the nights, at the weekends (as if he bloody well didn't suffer in the same jealous, atrocious manner, too), and her husband was wondering why she was so distant, and after all this new house meant so much to him, and the shopping at IKEA for new furniture and knick-knacks he kept dragging her to in his cheery insouciance, and it all made her feel so guilty, she explained.

If this was it, he said, give me at least one more night. He could see how torn she was, how despite all her best intentions, she couldn't bear to be the one to say it was possibly over. One night, he thought, and I will make love to her like never before and force a positive decision out of her. Not that he even believed himself. She agreed for the next day. Not tonight, her husband was doing the cooking at home and she was already late and he would be angry at yet another late night, and why was it that recently she had to work late so often, it wasn't like that before, was it?

The next day, her husband received an anonymous letter at work.

At seven o'clock, just as he was laying out the blanket on the office floor ready for her arrival, and sucking on Polo mints to freshen his breath, she rang. She was in tears, full of rage. It could only be him. What could he say? It all pointed towards him. Things in the damn letter that only he could know. He had once even joked about an envelope with her company's logo he had kept back, unused, from a note she had once given him at the pub. He wracked his brain in vain; sure, they hadn't really been taking too many precautions, hadn't always been discreet, but who? Her husband was an industrial journalist, could he have made enemies? Duplicitous friends who had pieced things together? Colleagues? Staff at his office who had assembled the clues of the puzzle together from his irrational behaviour, the stain on the sofa, the blanket, their regular telephone conversations? At any rate, she was heading home to save her marriage. She now hated him and nothing he could ever do or say would ever make her want to have any further contact with him again. He just stood there, paralysed, as she hurled abuse at him over the telephone line. He protested his innocence, too shaken to probably even sound convincing. The last time he saw her was standing at his building's door, the look in her eyes so withering, come to reclaim her letters and the two photographs she had once given him of her. He supposed they had been taken by her husband. Their memory remained etched forever in his brain. One with her hair short and uncurled, disturbed by what looked like a cold wind on the Beaubourg Plain in Paris, taken soon after her graduation from Cambridge. The other, just some months before he had met her, in the Northumberland countryside, her tousled hair almost orange, her eyes small and remote, wearing a black jacket, jeans and heavy DM shoes. A few months later, he took his courage in both hands and rang her at home on a day he knew she had taken off to catch up on manuscripts, and confronted her about this certainty she had that he was the sender of the letter. It turned out the letter was too well written and spelt difficult words correctly, as well as giving his private phone number. In her grief, this was now damning and incontrovertible evidence, it appeared. She made him swear to never write, call or try to see her again. Even threatening police action. He felt he couldn't fight. She was even now accusing him of a series of strange phone calls her husband and her had been getting for some months, conveniently forgetting they had begun long before their affair, as she had already told him about them then.

For a few months, his life fell apart.

Living with pain is a boring story.

He masturbated often, thinking of her endlessly and fishing up to the surface of his troubled mind desperate images of her body, stroke up, the look in her eyes, stroke down, the maddening curls of her hair, stroke up, the colour of her lips, stroke down, the moving shades of pink in her cunt when he chewed on her and his eyes immodestly peered deep inside. It didn't help much, but he managed to come, the white glue of his seed dripping into his fist.

Why does it have to hurt me, bruise me so? he reflected as he gazed at his drawn features in the small mirror in the toilet while he cleaned the mess off his hands. After all, millions have affairs, fall in lust, spiral in love, come apart. But at the back of his mind, an insidious voice also whispered that, somehow, some also did manage to stay together in the end.

Christmas and its desert of longing and loneliness. Then the February torment of Valentine's Day — would her husband send her a doggerel card, take her out for a meal, buy her flowers?

Came the time of writing stories again.

The Amputated Soul

– You know, I'm very angry at you.

– What have I done?

– You never even took any precautions, used a condom, asked me if I was on the pill.

– You're married, I'd somehow assumed.

– Well I wasn't.

– But your husband and you?

– We've always used condoms.

– Always?

– Yes.

– How bizarre. I know I have no right to say so, but it's a strange comment on the state of your marriage.

– Maybe. Anyway, I've gone on the pill now.

– And how have you explained such a momentous change to him?

– Well, buying the new house. It's going to be expensive, the new mortgage. He understands. Couldn't afford a kid right now. He knows I don't really want children.

– But does he?

– Yes, he does.

– I was still a virgin when I went to Cambridge. I'd misbehaved quite a bit before, but somehow I never did do it.

– And when was the first time?

– At University, at a party. This guy suggested we go together, and I decided, why not, and we just did. It was nothing special.

– And afterwards?

– I caught up for lost time. You know how it can be when you're a student, you're away from home for the first time. Don't think I was promiscuous, I wasn't really. There were only three other guys. And some of them didn't really last long. I met my husband in my second year. He was then going out with a friend of mine, and I was with another guy. But all our friends sort of said we looked good together. So it happened. There, you're only my fifth lover.

– I'm madly jealous of every man who touched you then, you know.

– I miss you awfully. So, anything interesting at the office today?

– They've finally agreed I could make an offer for that novel I was telling you about. I'm really excited. It won't be much money, but I hope the author accepts it. The book still needs some work done to it, but I think he will be willing to listen to my suggestions. He sounds a bit weird, but the novel is really good.

– I miss you. I thought about you all weekend, tried to imagine what you were cooking, when you were doing your shopping at Sainsbury. I can't seem to get you out of my mind.

– I know, I know.

– At one stage, I wanted to talk to you so bad, I even phoned.

– You didn't!

– Yes. He picked up, so I slipped on a Liverpudlian accent, and said 'Sorry, wrong number, mate'.

– That was you… He was fuming. He hates being called 'mate'.

– It's unfair. You always undress me first. Why can't it be the other way around?

– Sure.

– There you are. This is me. Look at me. I'm so much older than you. I'm a bit overweight. There's more and more grey in my hair and I can never comb it properly. And this is you, standing there, so beautiful. Shit, what do you see in me?

– I like your hair. The curls on your chest, it's wonderful.

– Here, put your hand on my cock. See how you make it grow so effortlessly. Just being with you gives me a hard on. I am in awe of you, of your nudity. Yes, squeeze it more. Yes.

– I like it when you give me orders. You can be so authoritative.

– It's the old managing director in me…

– The other night in bed, next to him, I just kept on tossing and turning so much. I had to get up and go to the other room to read. It was an old book I'd already read; I couldn't really concentrate. Dickens or Jane Austen, I think. My body ached for you so much, even though we had only parted a few hours before. Why is it so strong? I feel I just want to be consumed by you, eaten alive.

– I feel the same. I just hate the idea that ten miles away, some nights, he might be caressing you, making love to you, it almost makes me feel sick. That he invades you where the imprint of my cock still lingers inside you.

– I just can't make love to him after the time I spend with you. I'm not that wicked. Most times, by the time I get home, he's already sleeping.

– Jesus, I don't know how you do it. You're the best lover I've ever had.

– You're not just saying that, are you, because we're together right now? It's ever so dangerous. It's the sort of thing that's likely to stay in a man's mind forever. I'm touched. Deeply.

– No, of course not. You're also my first circumcised penis.

– Really?

– And you have so much hair on your chest.

– Yes, a proper monkey, that's me.

– At the conference, you know, I was sitting in the lobby on that Sunday morning hoping you would come across and see me. It was something about you. The way you read, the way you looked.

– Premeditation, hey?

– He hates it when I clip my fingernails in the bath. I don't know why, it's just so natural. Why should it bother him.

– I agree.

– He's so involved with his new job. He takes me for granted. He's a few years younger than me, and some times I feel he just sees me as a convenient substitute for his mother.

– And the sex?

– It's okay, I suppose. Not like in the early days, when we were together at Cambridge. We lived together for some time before we married. We almost didn't. We had some terrible rows. I have such a temper. I even throw things. See, you don't really know me.

– I wouldn't mind you throwing things at me, if it was a condition of living with you.

– Oh, it was nothing hard, just an old ham and tomato sandwich.

– Beware the mad sandwich hurler!

– We finally went to see *The Piano* yesterday night. It was good, as you said. There was a difficult moment. He remarked on the fact that we had never been to this particular West End cinema before, and I stupidly blurted out that I had, forgetting briefly it was with you. But he didn't make anything of it.

– Yeah, London's a dangerous city. Soon, too many bars, restaurants and places will become part of our own private geography. We have to keep both worlds apart.

– The whites of your eyes are so… white when you're above me, making love to me.

– They're nothing special, really.

– No, they are so white. Oh, look at the time, I have to go.

– Do you really want to?

– No. Some evenings, I just want to stay here in this office for-ever, with the candle light flickering over us. But I can't.

– Stay. I will become hard again and make love to you in every conceivable pornographic position, missionary, rear, side-ways, upside down, make you scream, groan, cry. Stay a little bit longer. God, how the tenderness is swelling inside of me and I feel I'm like some bomb, ticking away, that I desire and need you so.

– Why does lust make us feel that way?

– Because it was meant to be, I suppose.

– Jesus, Jesus, Jesus, I could let you do absolutely anything to me. I trust you implicitly. It's crazy.

– Would you let me put my fingers around your neck and squeeze gently until the pain comes? Would you let me distend the rim of your arsehole, making it more pliant so that I might in-sert myself there and fill you, mark you forever in that forbidden place? Look at my finger, you're already so wet down there. Lick it. See how I dip my finger in cunt and arse and sip your juices so naturally, so fragrant, my mistress, my lover.

– Yes, my lover.

– Come with me to New York. I want you for a whole week. I want to spend whole nights fucking you, worshipping you in strange hotel rooms. I want to wake up beside you, I want to smell your breath in the morning when you awake, I want to see your tired cheeks without make-up and the wrinkles of our love-making carved like a tattoo under the surface of your skin, all over the map of your body.

– You know I can't. How would I explain it? Anyway, you know I no longer have any holidays left at the office.

– I'm sure those are not love bites. I'm always very careful.

– Let me see in the mirror. No, it's just orgasmic flush.

– It's all over your neck and the top of your chest. What's he going to say when you get home?

– Don't worry, it will fade away…

– I know, I know.

A LONG LETTER TO K
(with apologies to Leonard Cohen)

*I obsess over you, K. Here I am at my typewriter,
unshaven for the last four days, all grey sharp stubble,
probably more than ever looking my age, in what has now
become my room, surrounded by the paraphernalia of my
life, the piles of books, countless magazines, record albums
and CDs, the mattress against the back wall, the reality of
what is left of me after your passage through my days.
Outside the window, a thin layer of frost whitens the green
manicured surface of the lawn, and the bare winter
branches of the trees. I wonder what you are doing right
now. Whether you are wearing your long skirt of many
colours which appeared so transparent with the sun in
your back that morning I picked you up in Camden Town,
outlining the dazzling shape of your legs, rising from
small black boots all the way up to the volcano of your
crotch. What perfume you are wearing; maybe one from
the amusing assortment of small fancy flasks I'd bought in
duty-free at Kennedy. When was the last time you even
thought of me, of our so few hours together? If you did
actually get around to buying that CD of Nanci Griffiths'
or finally got a raise at your job for the New Year. A trade
magazine revealed how much your boss was earning; yes,
you certainly deserved a better salary, considering. I miss
the sound of your voice, the drawn out 'Helloooo' when
you pick up the phone and I daily resist the temptation to
dial your number. The last time we did speak, you almost
suggested that I needed psychiatric assistance and why did
I have this compulsion to write you sordid letters? I had
no pat answer to give you. And that my lines, my sad
pleas caused you distress and could I not do the decent
thing and just fade away and let you get on with your life?
Understand me, I cannot. I have lost you, I know, but you
will not in your anger deny me the memories, the
tenderness of what we fleetingly possessed before events
and your sense of guilt and craving for respectability bid*

you throw it all away, handed as you were a perfect
excuse. You see, I am not a respectable person; I am
unbearably selfish. Well, what would you expect of a
romantic pornographer, you of all women with your cold
heart of glass and your passion for independence, secure in
the knowledge of your beauty and your damning pride.
But I am a good person, I assure you. You made me that
way. Earlier today, I was browsing through a collection of
photographs with a nice introduction by Jayne Anne
Phillips, The Last Days Of Summer. *Full of images of*
naked teenagers on far beaches, their bodies full of an
expression of innocence not lost by knowledge, luxuriating
in textures of sand, flesh, cloth, tide pools and gentle
waves. So call me a paedophile, then. I remembered how
much I would dream during our nights apart of taking
you to the sea, not just a sordid dirty weekend in
Brighton, but under some blazing tropical sun, where I
would see you for the first time in a bathing suit, your
fluid limbs sprawled akimbo in the light of the falling sun.
Or even a nude beach, where I would admire how natural
you would stand in the buff and would feel both proud at
how I was exhibiting your charms to the insidious gaze of
other men and jealous of the fact they could not be blind
and allow me the exclusivity of your voluptuous nudity.
Then I fantasised about how I wanted to adorn your
exposed flesh, setting a diamond in the jewel-case of your
navel, shaving your pubic hair away, setting clamps of
gold around your nipples and piercing your labia, to feel
the thrill of a ring dangling from the lips of your cunt,
twisting it under my tongue when I licked you, sucked
you, ate you, my cock rubbing against the metal that
would now be part of you every time I moved within. Silk
threads carefully wound around your neck, wrists and
ankles. Oh, K, I know you would have allowed me. And all
the places I wanted to take you. To a bed and breakfast in
old San Francisco at Christmas, with antique elevators
inside wrought-iron cages, to New Orleans for New Year's
Eve, to stand on the banks of the Mississippi river nearby
the Jackson brewery to listen to the hooting funnels of the
riverboats at midnight amongst the boisterous crowd and
later to cruise, plastic glasses in hand, down Bourbon

Street, past the wonderfully shameless topless and bottomless joints and myriad bars with overhanging balconies full of revellers and happy drunkards. I know this lovely hotel in the French Quarter, you see, where all the rooms are distant from the lobby building, old slave houses set in a circle around drooping vegetation, so private that I could allow myself to scream your name to high heavens when I come like a river inside you, and no one can hear the disturbing noise of my excess. Yes. A hotel room in Paris, on the Left Bank, on a top floor, with a vista of wet roofs and latticed metal gratings, where the walls are so thin you can't help listening to couples in neighbouring rooms making love with all the sounds of indecency. The Algonquin in New York, where the rooms are small but the furniture is delicately antique and breakfast can be taken outside in bagel places close by, where I would introduce you to the Jewish delights of garlic bagel with lox and cream cheese, a meal of kings in its own right. A beach under the fierce Barbados sun, staying in a cabin, licking away the grains of sand that have crept up inside your sex whilst on the beach, washing the crack of your arse clean of all impurities and wading out, both naked, to the water at midnight and admiring the shadow of a yellow moon illuminate your erect wet nipples. Or oysters by Puget Sound in Seattle. The world's best roast duck at the Water Margin in Golders Green, in North London. The human geography of pleasure unbound. See how I obsess. I take the Northern Line daily to my office, a lump in my throat when I pass Goodge Street and guess you might be alighting there from a train going in the opposite direction. Sometimes, I even get off at my own station and wait on the other platform if a train has stopped there, peering inside as it speeds away for a vision of you and your crazy curls on the way to your own job. When I wash in the morning, my mind wanders and imagines what you might be wearing that day, whether your fool of a husband made love to you the evening before, how in darkest hell he found deep inside himself the generosity to forgive you when he discovered the facts of our affair. And even when I try not to think of you, he then reminds me without fail when he appears on my television screen standing in some factory car park pontificating about the state of the industry on the regional news, or crusading for victims of Stock Exchange swindles in his cheap suit. Of course, I hate him, I move closer to the screen when he appears to peer at the landscape of his pimples — how the hell do they let him appear on the box with all those blemishes, look, there's a big red one near his eyebrow almost ready to burst! When we were still lovers, I feared him and noticing him for the first time during a live broadcast, I even thought him handsome in a bland sort of way. No longer, he looks like a clumsy amateur, a few more years and he will be hopelessly going to fat. But would I be any better for you, I ask myself? The pain of your absence is killing me softly, day by day, hour after lonely hour. Do you still listen to the Grant Lee Buffalo album I turned you onto? I've made a few other great rock discoveries since: the Walkabouts, Counting Crows. Somehow all these callow musicians manage to express so many of the things I seem incapable of with only the power of words. If only I had learned how to play an instrument when I was younger. So what more can I say, apart from repeating the boring litany of how I miss you and want you still? Oh yes, I'm no saint, I fuck other women, but I detest myself as I always feel compelled to evoke images of you when I am with these others, to help me stay hard inside them, to furnish me with the rage to plough my furrow of infamy inside their bodies. I feel sweaty, dirty, in these hurried embraces and my cock softens, so I close my eyes and think of the lunar expanse of your great arse, the delicate lack of opulence of your breasts, the jutting geometry of your hip bones, the heartbreaking pallor of your body. See how low I stoop. Forgive me. I have written you letters, yes, letters full of hate and anger, letters that made no sense, letters that bled and roared, but none of them were sent and I sit here imagining stories I might write one day. Tales of sound and fury where the red flowers of the mountain will scream Yes to the returning sailor home from the wars, where St Germain des Prés in Paris after WW2 will bear witness to the lovelorn passions of a group of expatriates Yes I might complete that novel about passions out of erotic control against a panoramic

landscape of mythical American highways and love on the
run taken to its orgasmic conclusion Yes or that crazy tale
of lovers who fuck themselves to death to explore what lies
on the other side Yes I obsess and the ghost of you is taking
over my life Yes my love. And I never ever saw you dance.
So, night falls and a cloak of darkness surrounds me, snow
is falling, Boston and New York airports are closed, and
the roads out there are treacherous and deadly. I imagine
myself in a car, blocked by the snowdrifts, with the
temperature falling, my breath visible in the restricted
space of this odd cockpit, even with gloves on my fingers
are becoming numb and outside there are no lights for
miles and miles. What a stupid way it would be to die like
this, just because I wanted to get away from you and
foolishly thought the road was the answer. So, I return to
London and now my life begins again, my mind still
engulfed in hopeless passion, buried in the folds of her
flesh, the dark brown vulnerability of her sad, married
eyes. Today is the first day of the rest of my life (or what is
left of it). I wonder what bodies will come my way again,
how will they compare? Will they shudder and hold their
breath back as she did when I slipped a finger inside the
pliable tightness of her anal aperture? I know they won't.

– Why, when you touch me, do you always seem to do all the
right things?
– I don't know, I suppose it just comes naturally.

71-73 Charing Cross Road

Dear Mr Jakubowski,

I feel compelled to write to let you know how much I enjoyed that book you selected for me. I didn't know that one could possibly laugh so much at the spectacle of some- one else's pain, but the sequence where the hood was attacked by the dog, and his later flight with its head still attached to his arm and the ensuing gangrenous folly was just too much. Hilarious.

I look forward to your next recommendation.

Yours sincerely,
Katherine Macher

Dear Ms Macher,

I hope you enjoy the enclosed. Another dark story of dogs but this time taking place in a hellish version of New York, rather than the semi-comic sleaze of Miami (which I actually visited recently on the occasion of a book fair).

It's a well-known fact that I'm no great animal lover, but I assure you that dogs are not at the top of my hit-parade of least lovable pets. Cats are. But sadly, cats in crime fiction are always endearing, cuddly and engagingly cosy. Maybe one day I should write a tale where unwelcome members of the feline species come to all sorts of grim and deadly exits?

Enjoy.

Best regards,
Maxim Jakubowski

Dear Mr Jakubowski,
You've hit the right nerve or funny bone again. I didn't realise there were so many uses for a dead dog!

I'm no cat lover either. Once, when I must have been seven or eight and temporarily living with my aunt, I developed a strong antipathy to her cat (I don't recall its name all these years later; why must pets always be given names, stupid ones at that? An absurd habit), and one evening fiendishly poured some turpentine into its milk bowl (I used to spend many of my leisure hours painting by numbers and was given a small bottle of turpentine to clean my brushes). Naturally, the next morning the cat was found belly up in the garden. My aunt, who lavished all her affection on the horrible thing, became madly emotional but I never came under suspicion. Thus, you might say, began my career in crime...

Yes, you should write a story where cats come to all sorts of horrible ends. It would be fun. I'd heard you wrote in addition to owning the bookshop, but have never read anything of yours. Do send me something. I'd love to read what another sworn enemy of the animal kingdom might conjure up.

Yours,
Katherine Macher

Dear Katherine,
Thanks for your letter.

It's been a long time since I've written any fiction I'm really satisfied with. And, fortunately, past mistakes are now out of print, so I shall have to disappoint you. Also, most of my past work has not been in the crime and mystery field. Mostly fantasy, doomed tales of love and death in other dimensions or imaginary worlds that were too often rather close for comfort and reminiscent of the all-too-realistic world that surrounds us, or rather me. All very self-centred, I must say in retrospect.

I do a lot of non-fiction, though. Writing on film, rock music and of course crime. Here's a remaindered copy of a recent critical effort, which won a prize in Canada of all places. It should be useful. Not all the books mentioned in it are still available, but do let me know if any sound interesting to you, and we can try and provide you with them.

Best regards,
Maxim Jakubowski

Dear Maxim,
I was shopping in Bellevue the other day (it's on the other side of the lake from Seattle; they have some good shopping malls there) and was browsing through this large bookstore full of old and used books. Somehow I'd remembered you telling me you had written fantasy. Lo and behold, on the first shelf I look at, there you were. A paperback copy of *Beyond Lands of Never*!

Your story touched me in strange ways.

Tell me about yourself, about London.

Yours,
Katherine

Dear Katherine,
What is there to say? I'm a book junkie through and through, I live surrounded by books both at the shop and home. They mean so much to me, and I collect madly, even when there is no longer space on my shelves and floors. There's no logic to it, even though I sadly know that I shall never get around to reading even a quarter of the books I hoard.

London is London.

The Charing Cross Road is a bookworm's paradise still, though some of the smaller, quainter bookstores have long moved on because of costs. I'm lucky these particular premises became available. Outside, it's spring already and both the weather and the women are in bloom, which puts joy in my heart, but tramps who reek of drink and piss at night on the doorstep darken the view. It's like another world, hidden behind the facade of the books, one where life and the recession act out their depressing charade, and so many people are out of work and pester you for money for booze, and gypsy women accompanied by round-faced children on the underground beg or pretend to be refugees from Bosnia, and pitiful buskers strum out-of-tune guitars and nasally serenade crowds with chainsaw massacre versions of *Norwegian Wood*. Sometimes, I just wonder.

I've asked Thalia in mail order to send you those John Dickson Carr locked room novels you'd enquired about some time ago. They've now come back into stock.

What about you?

Regards,
Maxim

Dear Maxim
London sure sounds interesting. Like all nice places, it has I see a dark side. Here, we have Capitol Hill, once bohemian and flowery, now grunge capital of the world, with men and women looking pale and miserable and proud to be ugly. It's the young men in their silly shorts and unattractive hairy legs even in the deep of winter who get to me. I can take the hair, the greyness of their clothes, but it's the legs, I can't help from giggling.

There certainly is a weird fascination about locked room mysteries. Surely lessons in how to commit the perfect murder and get away with it. Though some of Carr's plots are fiendishly complicated and unwieldy, to say the least.

Last weekend I went to visit friends who live three hours south in Portland, Oregon. I'd been to State University there with Lisa, we even shared an apartment for two years; now she's married to this French photographer who she swears is cheating on her. Jean-Paul had to go on some fashion assignment on Sunday morning, so Lisa suggested we go to this nude beach in the Willamette Valley. I was somewhat taken aback, it's something I'd never thought about doing ever before. But I was reminded of that character in that short story of yours who dreams of topless women on foreign beaches and the thousands of breasts on display in all shapes and sizes. So I said yes, why not? It was a weird experience, but pleasurable. There weren't that many people around. The beach was down in a deep canyon and the river level was very low. At first I felt self-conscious and remained only top-less, but close by there was a family with some young kids and it all looked so natural, so after an hour or so, I took my bottom off. A day to remember.

You're to blame, of course.

I want to know more about your London.

Love,
Kate

Dear Kate,
I feel pleased and confused that you're telling me so much of yourself.

Yes, I can imagine you on the nude beach, with green hills and mountains surrounding the river bed canyon. I close my eyes and turn to crime. A criminal voyeur of the imagination. I try to conjure up the image of your hair in the wind (long? Dark auburn shades?), the shape of your body, the curve of your breasts, the roundness of your buttocks. Yes, you must have looked quite beautiful and I accept the blame, all responsibility. It would have been nice to have been there, but then again I've been putting on weight these last years, and the spectacle might not have been as edifying, I fear...

London?

It's really unlike any other city. More like a collection of most diverse villages scattered together, with various focal points, the City for business, the West End for shopping and entertainment, Soho for food and now much neutered vice, parks and gardens galore, not many skyscrapers like American cities, all low-key, neutral, like a curtain that conceals shadowy truths. People often think of London as foggy, Dickensian, old. Not any more. It's a city with octopus-like extensions in all green directions, suburban, dull, exotic, safe, sordid, but for me still full of secrets.

And when the sun comes out the women are in bloom like nowhere else. Objects of fantasy, bodies of reality, voices, flesh.

I could imagine you here, you know.

But enough of my digressions...

I hope I haven't shocked you. Sometimes words escape and trap me. But it's better to be honest about it, I suppose. I get carried away on the waves of writing, letters, words take on a life of their own, move from brain to typewriter with too much ease. This is how I betray myself.

Kind regards,
Maxim

Dear Maxim,
No, you didn't shock me. Perhaps in a way I was secretly hoping you would be so direct. I understand. Really. Honesty can have its own rewards.

Listen. Or whatever one does when reading. I told you about my girlfriend Lisa, the one I went nude sunbathing with in Portland. You remember? Well, I'd told her that I was having this correspondence with you, that you wrote really sweet letters, so I suppose she remembered your name. So, the other morning, the post is dumped on the outside porch and I open the door and there was this thick envelope there. She'd found this book of yours for a few cents at Goodwill (it's a giant thrift warehouse, where you can find all sorts of crazy things), it's one you'd never told me about. She'd read it and said it was absolutely weird and disgusting, that I had to see it for myself.

Gee, my mind is still in a whirl. I'd never come across something that made me so randy before. Lisa says it's the bit about the cystitis and pissing all blue that grossed her out, but I didn't mind so much; well, it's sometimes a fact of life, isn't it, even if it's somewhat unpalatable? What got to me, though, was the bit about the ice. I'd never heard about anything like that before, for sure. I've got a healthy fascination and interest in all things sexual, well I've read a lot, put it that way, but wow! the ice sure freaked me out. And made me feel all funny. I'm horribly fascinated. Whenever I'm in the kitchen, I give the refrigerator strange looks, you know. In a perverse way, it's something I'd like to try just to judge what must be a curious mixture of pleasure and pain, but I'm sure it would be better with another, rather than alone, talk about solitary pleasures!

Did it ever happen to you, or as with all things bizarre did you read about it in a book and put it in your story?

I realise this correspondence is moving in strange directions. Forgive me.

Eager and curious for more.

Affectionately,
Kate

Dear Kate,

Well, *Rite of Seduction* is not a story I advertise too widely. You can understand why, can't you?

Sometimes I write things that I know are going to shock, even repulse people but I can't help it. It's part of me. You have a story you wish to tell, emotions you want to put across, feelings that call for a scream rather than a whisper, and it pours out because it's the thing to do, the way it is.

I write this, thinking of you in distant Seattle, half a world apart, excited in a million familiar ways because I realise I've established some form of connection with you, and I don't know where it's taking me.

All around, London is switching the sun off as summer nears its natural end, stronger grey winds building up, drizzly shards of rain cooling the temperature so that all the pretty unattainable women no longer display generous acres of flesh, bare backs, tan lines like necklaces above their shoulders, nipples almost bursting through their thin T-shirts, legs with no end peering out from the shortest of skirts or dresses. Enough. I obsess too easily. Control.

Imagine the newspaper headline:

LONDON BOOKSELLER GOES ON SEX CRIME SPREE
The owner of a specialist bookshop on London's Charing Cross Road was arrested today after making passes at every woman under the age of sixty that entered his shop. He says 'I just couldn't help it. They were all too pretty.'

You wouldn't forgive me, would you, Kate?
Confused,

Maxim
PS A real waste of a letter really, this. Maybe you should ignore it altogether. I seem to have rambled on in a most silly fashion.

Dear Maxim,

Maybe you should come to Seattle. After all, the World Mystery Convention is taking place here next year. Should you need an excuse? I want to meet you, and no, I don't know what will happen when we meet. I feel I know you so well already. Something about you scares me a little, but I'm ready, more than I will ever be. Yes, I too invent newspaper stories:

MAD SEATTLE WOMAN SLAYS BRITISH AUTHOR

A Kirkland librarian who had been corresponding for some time with a British author was discovered yesterday by a neighbour in a catatonic state. The body of English bookseller and writer Maxim Jakubowski, 48, was found in her bedroom. He had been sexually mutilated.

Katherine Macher, 28, when interrogated later, after recovering from her state of shock, confessed 'his sexual demands were too bizarre'.

A Seattle Times *reporter later contacted mystery critic Marvin Lachman about the deceased, 'His crime stories were so violent they were like the literary equivalent of a snuff movie,' he said.*

Seriously, though, it'd be great if you could visit (I'd defrost the fridge beforehand to avoid temptation!).

Some time back, you recommended James Crumley to me, but I never did get around to him. Here's a cutting (a real one) from our local paper; he's reading at the Elliott Bay Bookshop next month. Do you know Crumley personally?

Yours,
Kate

Dear Kate,

Yes, I did meet Crumley some years back at a crime festival in the French Alps. He's a terrific guy, drinks mightily, a bit like a Hemingway of the crime world. A rather frantic life, so *The Mexican Tree Duck* is his first novel in a decade, A genuine event. You must attend the reading. and if you have the opportunity give Jim my best regards.

Sexually mutilated? Tell me more. Morbid, moi? Not at all.

Well, in London we're used to that sort of thing, you know. After all, Jack the Ripper, shrouded in his Dickensian fog, was the first modern serial killer of note. In the shop, we also sell a lot of true crime books, not by personal choice I assure you, but there are bills to pay. The interesting thing is that so many of the more gruesome volumes, those with all the gory details about the killings and mutilations inflicted on women by psychos (mostly American) are bought by women. And don't ask me why. I don't think I wish to know.

By the way, I want a photograph of you. My imagination is running out.

Yours, stoically impatient.
Maxim

Dear Maxim,
Here you are.
Is this what you expected? Is this what you want?

Kate

Dear Kate
So this is you.
I don't know what I truly expected. Really.
Yes. You.
Allow me to imagine the shape of your body under the long skirt of many colours that you are wearing (is that Seattle in the background, or Portland?), daringly guess the pallor of your breasts, the feel of your skin under my fingers skipping a gentle light fandango, how your body would feel naked against mine, flesh pressed against flesh, the smell of your skin, my tongue tasting you, the ineffable sensation of entering you for the first time.
I read in a book the other day that it rains in Seattle nine days out of ten.
Oh, how your wet cascading hair falls over your shoulders. A mental movie against the screen of my mind, raging images of bodies aflame as the storm invades my teacup of a brain and heart. Soft, invisible to the eye, golden down in the small of your

back. A dark beauty spot just below the lower curve of your right buttock. A brown mole where your small breasts take birth. Not opulent is the way you describe them.

If you were in London right now, we would be having an affair. Sneaking into cheap hotels, hunting for lies and excuses to the deception. Stealing brief evenings, weekends in search of always more forbidden joy. Would the sex be good? Impossible to say. Feverish, sweaty, shockingly intimate.

Come to think of it, there must also be a London of lovers. A London most of us know little about. A city where the geography is human as well as physical, where I should discover bars which are quiet and discreet, and I could take your hand in mine, without acquaintances spying. Where there are dark streets where I might slip my hand under your shirt and caress your shadowy nipples to hardness, alleys where our crotches might rub against each other with impunity.

Strange how the vision, the topology of a city can change according to circumstances, like a parallel world that exists contiguous to the one we know as normal, invisible but so close. In this one I sell books and write you foolish letters where I reveal the worst of my hidden self, in the other London, we fuck wondrously, mingle juices and sweat in unknown beds and awake blearily in the grey morning with my cock still embedded in you, a familiar geometry of desire and lazy friction binding our bodies together in adulterous ardour (you are married, aren't you? Somehow I guess you must be, and of course you know I am too).

Kate, sweet sweet Kate, what are we to do?

With much affection.
Maxim

Dear Maxim,
We meet in London. Certainly it must be London, the dark London of my imagination, the one from all the books full of fog and dread, the city of a thousand chimneys and unending parks where all policemen are polite like in a novel by Agatha Christie, where all the freaks fix you with mad, staring eyes like in the Factory books of Derek Raymond.

So we come together at last.

Six o'clock in a private club in Soho. We order drinks, make small talk and barely hear each other over the din of the regulars. Drinks over, you suggest we eat. We find a nearby Indian restaurant. The food is truly delicious. Then, a million things still unsaid, we move on to a pub. I imagine it's in a basement. Clumsily, we try to explain our feelings, how we arrived at this crazy situation. Fleetingly you touch my thigh through the fabric of my dress. I buy the next round. What I don't say is that you're not quite the man I expected. Your hair is flecked with grey, you readily admit you're slightly overweight. You're probably thinking, she never said she was so tall, and your eyes can't keep away from the small brown mole there at the onset of her cleavage.

'I'll drive you back to your hotel,' he suggests as closing time approaches. 'My car's in a car park just round the corner.'

'Yeah,' she answers. 'That's no problem.'

The West End theatre crowds were in the midst of their daily exodus and it took another fifteen minutes to climb the serpentine path up the concrete bunker. At one stage, she gently put her hand on his, but the vehicle in front moved a yard or two, and he had to move his hand to disengage the handbrake.

Strange how odd moments can live forever in your memory.

A touch of affection.

The blinding sound of yearning, of longing.

Outside the hotel, she kissed him lightly, between lips and cheek.

'We'll have to talk again,' she said.

'Yes,' he agreed.

And here my imagination fails me. How do we end the story, Maxim? Does Kate pull a knife from her handbag and stab him to death, blood spurting in all directions over the wet, shiny London street? Or, in a fit of despair, knowing they have nowhere else to go from here, does Maxim gently put his fingers around Kate's neck and strangle her? It's what characters in his stories would do, isn't it?

We both know too well there can be no happy ending, no desperate thrashing of bodies in hotel beds, sheets strewn to all poles, shrieks of orgasm equalling cries of death, no post-coital tenderness as fingers now explore opposite orifices with gentle care rather than brutal passion.

Tell me. Write me another ending.

Send me a mystery book where you don't come to Seattle to camp on my doorstep, quarrel with my jealous husband and end up badly beaten up by the younger man. Where I arrive in London to see you and learn you were killed when two black armed robbers attacked the store on a Monday morning, looking for the Saturday takings.

No, you will not come to Seattle and I will not go to London.

And delete my name and address from the shop's mail order records (and thank Thalia and the staff for the excellent service this past year).

So be it.
Kate

Wondrous Kate,
So farewell then. By the way, I never did find out what colour were your eyes.

Sadly.
Maxim

A cool morning in the American Northwest. Kate moves lazily from bedroom to bathroom, her long white night-dress trailing behind her on the wooden floor. Somehow, she senses that her state of mind is at last serene, appeased. She looks up at the small, square mirror of the medicine cabinet. She appears tired, she thinks. Her mind wanders, aimlessly. Her husband is away on a business trip; he is a financial journalist. She has the whole apartment to herself. She can't remember the last time this happened. Today is a day off from the library. There are pale, darker shadows under her eyes, she peers closer into the cabinet mirror. Her eyes are dark brown. Soon, she and her husband (who often ends up sleeping on the sofa at night after they have pointless rows) will move into their new house.

In London, eight hours time difference, Maxim wearily moves from bathroom to study, sighing, more flecks of grey in his daily growth of beard. The hell with it, today he doesn't want to shave. Downstairs, the sounds of the kids readying for school. He pulls the old red Atlas out from one of the bulging shelves. America. Washington State. Oh yes, north of Oregon. Seattle, there it is. He gazes absently at the colours on the map, the blue of the Pacific, immense all the way to Russia, the brown and white of the mountains, the green of the Montana open country. Christ, it's so far, he thinks. Far, much too far from London, naturally.

The Man Who Looked Like Mel Brooks

*'Maxim Jakubowski… acts like the perfect Englishman but
looks like a long-haired version of Mel Brooks.'*
The Big Issue, June 1994.

Golders Green: Other Men's Women

Though his outward appearance, standard-issue romanti-
cally morose, seldom betrayed him, the man who looked
like Mel Brooks was bitterly unhappy. There was this married woman, you see, and he just could not get over her. He sat at
his office desk, silent, lost in memories, scratching his ear-lobe
and, sometimes, a newly-acquired disgusting public habit,
tweezed out a superfluous hair from his ear, and cursed, raged,
cried inside. On a Thursday night, four months or so into their affair, they had made love with a fervour that had surprised both of
them. 'You're the best lover I have ever had,' she had said. 'I just
don't want to go back to him tonight,' she had said. 'I want to stay
here forever.' Yes, she said, she said. But the last train from
Charing Cross station beckoned, and she had caught it. Network
South East to the small house she and her husband had just purchased. Over lunch at the Spice of Life pub the following
Tuesday, she told him she had kept on thinking of him throughout the weekend, and the pain and guilt were becoming unbearable. 'So, choose me, come to me,' The Man Who Looked Like
Mel Brooks had proposed. 'But I have a cold heart, I am foul-tem-
pered, I just can't understand what you see in me,' she had
replied. 'I am in sheer awe of your naked body,' he had said.
'Please, please, you must stay with me; the things you do, the

things you say touch me deep inside, you know. It can never be the same again, you realise.' By Wednesday, however, it was all over. Maybe her husband had somehow found out. Two evil letters in the Royal Mail, and a final vision remained inside him of her dark-brown eyes lost in the wondrous desert of her blonde curls, piercing his heart as she stampeded towards him to retrieve her letters and unfairly blamed him for the whole fiasco. 'I can never forgive you for this,' her pride and unjustified anger said to him. So, sometimes you think it's the end of the world, but reality sure has a way of trivialising the melodrama, and you keep on living, of course, but all around you the emptiness of London can become so bloody overwhelming. He still wants her so badly, wishes to see her, to touch her anew, to hear her again (what is she reading? listening to? wearing? how did the wisdom tooth operation go?) but she has threatened a legal injunction should he try and contact her again. The Man Who Looks Like Mel Brooks thinks of spiteful revenge, his mind aglow with mischievous plotting. He now believes she has used him just to add some spice to the failing sex life of her marriage. He will get his own back. A throwaway paragraph in Frederick Forsyth's latest novel provides him with an idea.

Blackheath: The Husband Who Took His Wife For Granted

The woman who once cared for The Man Who Looked Like Mel Brooks lies restless in the conjugal bed in the upstairs, sparsely decorated bedroom of a south-London semi-detached with an ornamental goldfish pond in the back garden. She ponders the future. Next to her, on the left side of the bed, her husband snores gently. She feels her life is being made a misery, her ex-lover still writes her feverish, unreasonable letters and tries to contact her, which only serves to remind her of what she now feels is the worst mistake she has ever made, while on the other hand she cannot banish from her senses all those good moments, the lust, the tenderness, the sweat-drenched encounters, the shocking white of his eyes as he moved in and out of her and she couldn't help herself from screaming 'Jesus, Jesus' out loud. Why can't he stop pestering her thus, she is no longer interested in him, what does he want, for her to leave the country? Today she bruised her inner thigh again on the sharp corner of her desk; her favourite horror writer has moved away to another publishing house and she fears that many of the other writers she is nurturing will soon do the same as the publisher she works for just cannot promote their books properly; she even suspects her erstwhile lover of bad-mouthing her among literary agents. Outside, the sun is shining hot today, she guesses he is probably wearing his perennial black T-shirt, down there in the West End, just a few miles away. Oh, why can she just not banish him from her mind? He worries her, he's so unpredictable, what is he going to do next? She remembers his wonderfully pornographic letters, that fax he briefly feared he had transmitted to another machine on a separate floor of her office, the flowers and the books, the music tapes and the perfume he would give her. The way he could always surprise her. The bastard. Every time she now makes love with her husband, she can't help mentally comparing how it was with him. Better, but so what? How his long, unruly hair swept down over her face, how white his eyes shined. She recalls the way he touched her, always right, the look on his face, the hair on his chest and back, the energy, the smell of his breath, the despair. Now it's a painful memory, but she remembers the time when she would have allowed him to do absolutely anything, and he did: never before had a man bound her hands, coloured her nipples and nether lips with the scarlet shade of her own lipstick, slipped his whole fingers where he had, circled her neck with his outstretched hands. Why does she now hate him so? It was only sex, after all. It was good while it lasted, sharpened her libido at a time when her husband was too busy with thoughts of his own career at the BBC. Couldn't that have been enough for him? What did he expect, more?

Goodge Street: The Imaginary Life

Another day, another planet. In this world, The Man Who Looks Like Mel Brooks thinks he's happy at last. There's one born every minute, as the saying goes. He awakes in the morning, always at six, a willing slave to his biological clock, often still embedded in her. He watches her breathe as she sleeps in the nude while the weather still allows, gazes at the invisible remains of a childhood scar on her right cheek, slips a distracted finger through the tangle of her Medusa curls, observes the swell of her throat with every intake of air, the way her pale chest moves up and down again in rhythm with the beating of his waiting heart. He listens to the silent melody of her beauty, a fly on the wall of her sleeping consciousness. He pulls the cover away from her impossibly long body, marvels at the texture of her bare skin, the flatness of her stomach, the ever-present bruises on her thighs, like a camera he memorises every square inch of her, the vast expanses of her nudity, every single mole and blemish. the lunar horizon of her beautifully large hips. She opens her eyes, blinks at the early sunlight filtering through the thin curtains of the flat, focuses slowly still without the assistance of her contact lenses. 'You know,' she tells him. 'That journalist got it completely wrong, you don't look like Mel Brooks at all. Apart from the fact that you fart in bed, as he probably does, and you're both Jewish, there is no similarity at all.' He smiles. 'Just fellow members of the circumcision club, I suppose. A woman in France many years ago actually said I looked like Charles Aznavour, go figure.' She laughs; he watches her and melts inside. They go to a ball at Hatfield House on a warm summer evening. He insists she wears high-heels and her long black party gown, with that garter belt and bustier set of hers that just drives him crazy. She protests that with high heels she will tower over him and other guests and will feel too self-conscious. But he orders her to go that way. She lowers her eyes in obedience, revelling in the submissiveness. As she alights from their red car, the falling sun shines heroically through the fabric of the dress, highlighting the glorious silhouette of her stockinged, unending legs. He gets a hard-on.

Away-Day To Brighton: Just Another Sordid Story

The Man Who Looked Like Mel Brooks had always dreamed of directing a movie. He wouldn't have minded penning *The Producers*, even though he tends more towards irony than belly laughs, but *Vertigo*, *Le Feu Follet* or *Liebestraum* are more in his league: his familiar cocktail of death, obsessions and *amour fou*. He's a writer, so he sits at his word processor, dark blue screen and cursor flickering, and composes his dream movie. In it, she moves through the city, along the London streets he knows so well, with her childlike face surrounded by wild blonde curls, insouciant like Julie Christie in *Billy Liar*, her brown suede waistcoat flapping in the breeze. He closes his eyes. His soul on fire has an ache in it like cracked leather. Damn the budget, he decides, and opts for a foreign location. Here, she skips through the Oregon mountains catching the Aurora Borealis illuminating the horizon over Vancouver Bay. All romantic movies need a lush soundtrack, so he pulls out CDs by Erik Satie, Grant Lee

Buffalo, Leonard Cohen, The Walkabouts, Counting Crows and The Pogues' *Tuesday Morning* from the crowded racks that surround his desk and plays the music loud enough to drown the demons inside, the sound of his despair. On the screen, the celluloid frames move faster and faster. Now, she walks naked through an Identikit hotel room, like in Brighton on the eve of the Labour Party Conference when they had spent a whole 24 hours together united by the flesh, migrating from bed to bath to floor to bed again, while outside the camera crews were setting-up and he had been absurdly reminded of her damn husband, whose crowning television hour had been a report on the state of the British condom industry, filmed at a freezing seven in the morning in the car park of an Essex factory. He orders the cameraman to increase the focus, so that all the spots and pimples on her husband's face are highlighted even further. 'Don't be petty,' she says as she moves in beauty to the table where she had left her handbag and, left handed, pulls a tube of cream from it, 'Come, I'll give you a massage.' The Man Who Looks Like Mel Brooks obeys, interrupts his home movie and lies down on the bed to await her ministrations. She stands between him and the curtained window that hooks out on the sea front, and her white Irish flesh appears diaphanous to him.

Heathrow: The Secrets Of Geography

Please, please, do not write to me, fax me, write more stories about me, she writes to The Man Who Looks Like Mel Brooks. You are causing me distress and pain. But writing is remembering, he wants to tell her, and I love you to death, worship the ground you walk on. On the other hand, he cannot bring himself to forgive her for the rejection, the web of lies she has no doubt spun around her husband to deny there ever was an act of adultery, this other guy's just crazy, just ignore him, he can hear her say. She lies well, he knows. He slips on a black shirt and drives off toward south London. The first frost of the year shines over the empty roads at four in the morning. He crosses the river near the National Film Theatre. In New Cross, he spies a 7-Eleven convenience store open and purchases sugar in a half-pound bag, together with a couple of morning papers and a Kit-Kat bar to assuage his early hunger. The poison is rising inside him. He remembers her once mentioning that her husband was a vegetarian. He sneers with undisguised contempt. A spotty vegetarian journalist from up north with a worthless degree in history from Cambridge. He targets his inner rage. He's always supported Oxford in the boat race anyway. The bastard just doesn't deserve her. There's almost no traffic. He races down Lewisham Way, reaches the Lewisham Road intersection and takes Belmont Hill which itself changes into Hill Lee Terrace. After Blackheath station, he continues east on Blackheath Park. Almost there. He takes a right turn and parks on Brooklands Park. Sugar in the pocket of his leather jacket, he briskly walks back to Blackheath Park. Shortly before the sports ground he spies their road, pretentiously masquerading as a mews. He looks around. No one. Just some mist ahead under the greenery. It's a small street. They moved here a year ago, from a claustrophobic apartment just three streets away. They've borrowed heavily, even from her parents, made a loss on the flat, the old negative-equity game. He recognises the car parked outside the smallish house. It's all they can afford, years old, lets in the water when the rains are too heavy, but he needs it for work, to travel to the various studios as the Corporation refuses to provide. The windows of the house are uniformly dark. He tries not to think of them lying together in the bed upstairs. How this other man, this legal man of hers, touches her, smells her, lives with her frightening intimacy. He moves to the car and unscrews the petrol tank cap. It has no lock. With a quick look around to check the coast is still clear, The Man Who Looks Like Mel Brooks enjoys his vengeance as he pours the whole bag of sugar into the tank. He replaces the cap with a last gaze at the silent upstairs bedroom window, and feels a bitter knot in his throat. He moves away. Morning is rising. Why doesn't he feel better now?

Bow Street Magistrates' Court: Evil Never Triumphs

The Man Who Looked Like Mel Brooks whispered 'Forgive me' under his breath, as the young policeman, who didn't look a day over 18, asked him to accompany him. He had spoken so softly that the cop thought he actually said 'Guilty'.

Six In The Morning

He was headed towards middle age in low gear, going nowhere in no particular rush. Life was easy, rather quiet, unspectacular. He candidly thought he had left all the storms and the rage well behind by now.

And then she came into his life with no word of warning.

Eddie of the tousled blonde hair, the long white legs, the crooked teeth, the wide child-bearing hips, the dark brown eyes that looked at him with their peculiar mixture of wonder, interrogation and vulnerability.

An ill-advised letter, a few drinks, an Indian meal and a torrid episode of flesh against flesh in his empty office after dark, and he was soon a prisoner of the republic of desire, an almost-forgotten world of the excitable past, where he felt like a college kid all over again waiting for the phone to ring to hear her voice: 'Hello, it's Eddie', girlish, shy, bashfully lustful.

Her blondness eternal.

The hours, the days spent apart from her felt as if they lasted ages, thinking in silence of all the things she might be doing out there in south London. What she was wearing, how much her husband touched her in bed — he had already ascertained in conversation that she usually wore nothing to sleep, and the thought both excited him wildly and fanned his jealousy.

Over a Bank Holiday, she went to stay with her parents, and he imagined her frolicking beautifully in a Surrey garden of polished lawn and carefully pruned roses, back at night alone in the room she had grown up in as a child, and then as a rebellious adolescent, with her long-abandoned scruffy dolls as sole companions. He would close his eyes and feel like crying, as the lust grew so overwhelming, as it mingled deceitfully with the fear of ever losing the little he possessed of her.

A long weekend without seeing her, alone with his thoughts, sunny, unending days looking for things to do to carry his mind elsewhere, away from mental images of her face, her body.

Criminal Scenario One

Life has worn him down slowly. A marriage of affection, where both partners are now weary of each other's foibles, jobs lost, mortgages, claustrophobic rooms, bright but rebellious pig-headed children who insist on answering back. When he grows all too easily irritated with his family, it reminds him awfully of the way his father was with him when he was a teenager. Eddie is there outside, flying luminously through his other life, and he feels he must act, do something. He reads in the newspaper of a murder in Oxford of all places, shades of Inspector Morse. He kills wife and children with a hammer. The blood is everywhere. Now I am free, he says.

Sunlight slivering through the drawn curtain of the window of an anonymous chain hotel room near Charing Cross station. Eddie on her side, her flank partly in shadow, the oval shape of her breast rising gently over the sandy dunes of her body. An image he memorises for ever. A still life of his lover embedded in his neural circuits like the flash of a thousand cyberpunk suns.

He sort of wonders what he's got himself into. How does one conduct an affair, what are the ethics, the etiquette, the sheer human mechanics of extramarital liaisons?

He's read too many novels. He feels he's trapped in a bad story. He knows that with Eddie it's very special, but then again they would think that, wouldn't they? All illegal couples do. And the flies on the wall are probably falling over themselves laughing at the absurdity of the situation and the desperate seriousness they have made their own. Classic fools all.

He sees himself as a figure of ridicule. The archetypal middle-aged guy who has fallen for the sweet smile of some young bim-bette. Lolita redux. She is, after all, twenty years younger than him. But no, he tries to convince himself, she is different. He can feel it inside, remembering how when they lay together, cradled against each other, she would gently kiss his upper chest, while her cold fingers skimmed over his shoulders.

They don't know where they are going. It's an open boule-vard of dreams, like an American highway in those road movies he likes so much. 'We'll see how it goes. Take one step at a time,' they assure each other, grasping for reassurance. They swear they do not wish to harm, to hurt others through their irresponsi-ble actions, but she says he turns her on so much, does all the right things, and he just can't get her out from under his skin, he's literally entranced by her natural, unassuming, beautiful spell.

He should be suffering from scruples, feeling all sorts of deep and tortured remorse, but some days he just feels light-headed, serene, surprised he can shoulder the guilt so lightly.

What comes next?

Criminal Scenario Two

On a 6.23 train from St Pancras to Nottingham to a conference he would much rather not attend, he meets this strange guy who insists on starting a conversation. The stranger pulls a gleaming metal liquor flask from his coat and pours him a perfect shot of malt whisky. Later past Leicester, relaxed, it all comes out, how he wishes his life would change but this other woman he's going out with is married, and so is he and he doesn't know what to do. The stranger on the train suggests they do it like in the movies. You will take care of his wife, and he her husband. And you only have to do it once. Two for the price of one, hey? A bargain. Almost amused, he provides the unknown guy with respective names and addresses.

The longer the clandestine affair went on, the more being apart from her felt unbearable. One-sided telephone conversa-tions when one adulterer or another could not really say much, because of others standing around in their open-plan offices, would just add to their mutual frustration; snatched drinks in crowded pubs and hotel bars populated by inebriated foreign businessmen; unending weekends spent torturing each other with thoughts of what the other might be doing a few miles away across the river; meeting mutual work acquaintances and burst-ing to tell them the truth, all the truth just to see the look of sur-prise on their face at the idea of him and Eddie being together: 'No, surely not, I didn't know you even knew each other. But what about…'

The pace of their passion quickened. Barely a few hours after making love in some forbidden place, both would, independently of each other, clumsily inserting themselves back into the real world, yearn like crazy for the other, bodies crying out during the crowded night in the company of loving ones, once genuinely cared for.

They were coming together in sheer overdrive, losing control of the situation, their feelings, their day-to-day lives. Scared, confused, elated, depressed.

Monday mornings were often the worst, separately emerging from a weekend of missing madly, assaulted by doubt, by the possibility that something might have happened somehow to pull them apart, bringing spouses back into the eternal equation. A telephone conversation was then enough, reassuring like a warm blanket; checking that the miracle telepathy had worked again, they had been thinking the same things, feeling the same painful emotions, suffering the same irritations about the pettiness of the world and all it contained.

They would feverishly make plans, to steal an evening, a whole night, only to come crashing against the same old wall of fear. 'No, this is going too fast, we've only known each other eight weeks, we must slow down, be less intense, act like the grown-ups we know we are.' But their senses scream out a different tune, and they know they are just kidding themselves. This is a road to nowhere; impulsive, out of control, he knows that should he perhaps step on the brakes, the whole edifice will come crashing down over him like a wall of flames.

Criminal Scenario Three

Her husband gets an anonymous letter in the mail. 'Your wife is cheating on you. Where do you think she is on those evenings when she gets home so late? And that weekend at the TV symposium in Leamington Spa when she didn't want you to come and join her for the Saturday night?' it says, in a square old-fashioned manual typewriter face she cannot recognise. He is shattered, angry, badly hurt. Eddie responds blankly to the accusation, as surprised by the turn of events as he is. This is not the way she wanted it to be. She wonders who it can be. That woman in the office who's never liked her? But how could she have found out? Or was it her lover himself his patience eroded by the combined assault of all the hours they have not managed to spend together desperately attempting to precipitate events? Her husband walks out of the cramped, claustrophobic flat, drives off in to the south London night in a rage. Ten minutes later, he rushes through an orange light near Blackheath Park and collides with a heavy goods lorry which had right of way. He dies instantly.

He is in awe of her naked body.

As she sheds her black dress slowly, revealing the sheer Irish whiteness of her flesh, he gazes at the amazon beauty of her body.

Her hair tumbles like a blonde fountain around her pale face, undomesticated Medusa-like curls reaching across her forehead to her deep-set brown eyes. Her mouth is a slash of red lipstick, lips thick and sensual, ripe forbidden gates to her teeth and throat, to the distinct smell of her breath. The sleeve slides down across her right shoulder, unveiling the length of her arm. Her brassière is sheer black gauze cupping her breasts in delicate bondage; she slips it off and her nipples harden slightly under the strange caress of the cold ambient air.

His gaze moves lower to her navel. Her stomach is flat, like a marble table, the straight cliff of her belly descending like a sheer precipice towards her pubic area, where her thatch is much darker, curling wildly at the edges and projecting thick tufts at its centre, which he will have to part later to reach the unencumbered lips of her cunt to reveal the pink, obscenely textured walls of her moist sexual innards.

Her high pelvis circles out slowly in languorous curves from hips up to stomach, her unending legs beginning their journey downwards from its equator. Others might argue that her rear is too big, ever so slightly out of proportion, even to her tall frame, but he doesn't care in the slightest. He finds the whole lavish spectacle of her wondrously attractive, luminous even. He feels she was born to be nude like this; she should be painted, her long limbs spread-eagled over white drapes in pornographic poses; if only he knew how, he would take a hundred photographs of her, for private consumption, close-ups of her thighs which bruise so easily, enlarged studies of the pale brown moles and small beauty spots criss-crossing the ocean of her white skin, one slightly above the left breast, another at the onset of her cleavage, yet another beneath the right shoulderblade; yes, Polaroids of her toes, of her half-open scarlet lips revealing a few teeth out of conformist alignment, of the puckered hole of her arse when she lies down on the bed on her stomach and opens her legs and rear to his exploratory caresses.

She has a manly walk, a gawky posture, but he adores the way she strides nude from bed to bathroom, the way her hips swivel as she turns to avoid the corner of the bed and another bruise.

Her body, her soul, an object of desire.

'I missed you.

'Me too.'

'You look great.'

'Flattery will get you everywhere. Come here, hold me, I want you inside me.'

And he moves towards her, as nervous as the first time in his office. He wipes the red away from her lips, delicately twists the wedding and engagement rings off her finger, picks up her handbag from the floor, opens it and pulls out the golden-coloured lipstick tube and mashes the tip gently against her nipples; if he isn't capable of painting her portrait, at least he can adorn her breasts the colour of blood ruby.

Criminal Scenario Four

He returns home late one night after sex with Eddie. Following their exertions, they had washed as best they could at the minimal office sink. He is tired, his back hurts from the embraces on the hard floor and he goes straight to bed, forgetting to shower. His wife joins him soon, after completing the administrative update on the files she will require at tomorrow's surgery. He is dozing, half in reality, half in dreamland, she takes his hand to kiss him goodnight and smells Eddie's cunt still lingering on his fingers. Immediately, she feels violently sick. They have a flaming row. She makes dire threats. The next morning, while she is still sobbing in the bedroom, he feels he has no alternative and quietly walks over to the garage where he drains the hydraulic fluid from the brake system. There is a steep hill running downwards on the way to his wife's practice.

You've read all about in books, newspapers and magazine articles in the lifestyle sections. You've seen so many movies. You thought it was easier than this. You were damn wrong.

How in late twentieth-century contemporary London do married folk engineer affairs of the heart or of the body electric? How do they manage it? According to published statistics and reputedly accurate surveys, he and Eddie were not the only ones involved in this ridiculous game; there were supposed to be a million or so others out there, also lying, deceiving, being furtive and madly discreet, conducting the precise business of crazy passions and also thinking it didn't show on their face, in their eyes. Surely, all these other sexual adventurers planned things better. But where do you purchase the right book of adulterous etiquette? With the dos and don'ts, the handy tips, the practical explanations, the coded map revealing in which public spots it is possible to kiss openly and not be recognised by acquaintants, the welcoming bars or cafés willing and able to harbour illicit lovers, the pubs where the muzak doesn't play too loud and drown the sweet nothings and the frequent embarrassed silences. He would have paid a fortune for such a book of revelations. She would willingly have commissioned a documentary programme on its rationale.

It was like learning to walk all over again.

You thought clandestine sex was easy. It isn't. You must beware of not biting her in the throes of passion when the only impulse coursing through your body is to consume her in one gulp, to bring her closer in an act of gentle violence, chewing on the flesh of her breast, digging your fingers into the pillowed softness of her thighs (remember, she bruises easily), nibbling the taut skin of her neck. No bites, no marks.

You must remember, after washing the sweat, the dried come, the smell of her off your body in the kitchen sink out there in the office corridor, the grimy one which the office tea-lady normally uses for cleaning the mugs, to dress so carefully again in the penumbra. Beware of putting your socks on again inside out, of not hooking her brassière at the back together again as it was when her husband helped her dress that very morning. And what else might you have forgotten? Think. Hard. This is a dangerous road you're treading, my boy.

This is how you enter the twilight world of sin.

You find a small hotel in Bloomsbury towards the back of the British Museum, and you both blush intensely when enquiring whether they have a day rate. Both holding your mostly empty attaché cases like talismans of probity. You know the receptionist knows. Eddie blushes even deeper, a red hue of guilt painting her pale white skin from forehead to cheeks. Or it's a bed and breakfast in south Clapham, where the carpet on the stairs smells of cheap cologne, and you must both use a pay-phone in the entrance hall to call respective offices and beg off sick for the day.

Naturally, you always pay cash. Credit card vouchers, and of course later monthly bills, are a dead giveaway. Aren't they?

But they were fast learners, oh yes, they were.

And whenever the need grew so intense he couldn't bear it any longer, he would wait in ambush at ten to nine in the morning in the side street round the corner from her office, and surprise her striding jauntily towards the television station from her tube exit. Seeing him, she would lower her eyes, in false modesty.

'I want you badly Take the day off,' he would order.

Sometimes she would, sometimes she just couldn't. An important meeting, a visitor, a screening. But most times she would.

Criminal Scenario Five

The affair with Eddie is now two and a half months old. They have managed seven carnal encounters. He is an inveterate list-maker, he checks in his office diary the coded entries: over the course of their days and early evenings he has penetrated her sixteen times. Every time they part, it just gets harder to let her go. He wants her totally, selfishly. One autumn evening when it's already dark by six or thereabouts, he lurks outside the financial newspaper where her husband works. He recognises him from a photograph he had glimpsed in her handbag while she was in the hotel bathroom putting her make-up back on. He follows. Through wet streets on to the suburban train from the railway station. When the moment is right, shortly after the station, in the shadow of Blackheath Park, he hits him from behind with a steel bar he'd earlier found in the corner of his garage. The husband is taller, but he has the benefit of absolute surprise. Dazed by the first blow, her husband slips to the ground. Once there, he no longer stands a chance. Overwhelmed by thoughts of Eddie's childish face, he hits him again and again with the improvised weapon, kicks him violently in the stomach, in the head. Soon, the husband is no longer moving. Or breathing. He steals his wallet to make it look like a routine mugging.

'It's usually at six in the morning when I wake up and the house is all silent, that the pain is at its worst,' he tells her in an Italian coffee bar at equal distance from their respective offices. Once you deduct seven minutes' walking time each way, they have barely three-quarters of an hour left to talk to each other before the lunch break is over. She cradles a hot cup of cappuccino. He nibbles a plate of tuna salad. She lowers her eyes.

'I know, sometimes I wake up three or four times at night, thinking of things, of you,' Eddie replies. 'I just don't want you to be unhappy because of what is happening.'

'Okay,' he admits, 'sometimes I am unhappy, even bloody miserable, but then again I wouldn't want to exchange the few good times, when we are together, for anything else in the world. I'll accept the pain and the misery, it's still worth it, Eddie.'

'What are we going to do?' she asks him.

'I don't know.'

'You know, there are times in the morning when I'm on the commuter train coming into town, I sort of wish, dream that I might impulsively do something crazy, jump on to another train, go to India, leave everything behind.'

'I know the feeling,' he confirms. 'I want to go away too, take you with me and damn the rest of the world. I want to take you to New York, book into the Algonquin where the rooms are too small but the old furniture is nice, walk out into the winter cold of Madison Avenue and treat you to bagels and lox for breakfast. Later, we'd walk down to the Village and spend hours foraging in the basement of the Strand for cheap review copies of new books, have lunch off Bleecker in a Mexican restaurant. I can imagine you naked in the Algonquin room, Eddie, a silly game show on the silent television screen, the curtains drawn and your body all mine.'

'Sounds nice,' she says, 'but there's just no way I can get away for a whole week, you know that. And neither can you.'

He sighs. 'Or New Orleans, where the drunkards roil down Bourbon Street holding their plastic beer glasses, and the riverboats are docked on the Mississippi near the Jackson Brewery. Or Paris, where there must be a hotel on the Left Bank where the lift to the upper floors would barely be large enough to accommodate the two of us. Yes, couscous meals, and good wine, and you and you and you.' He smiles kindly, warming to the idea of their dreams of escape.

She looks up from her cup. Her long fingers move to his hand over the table-top, brush lingeringly over his lower arm.

'Jesus, Jesus,' she says.

Criminal Scenario Six

Although he has promised Eddie he will never do anything rash, the anxiety, the impatience are just gnawing away at the fabric of his gut, like a plague rat on the rampage. One evening, he is sitting morose watching golf on TV, when his wife walks into the room and complains that his socks smell. He hasn't bothered putting his slippers on since his return from the office. The sheer pettiness of her irritation bugs him. He ignores her remark. Soon they have a major argument on their hand. It inevitably veers out of control and when he least expects it, he somehow blurts out the existence of his affair with Eddie (although he is careful not to mention her by name, even though his wife has never met her or heard of her). The recriminations continue for hours. That night, while he is sleeping, exhausted by the pressures and their release, his wife quietly goes out by the back door to the garden, locks herself in the garage, connects a rubber hosepipe to the Volvo's exhaust and commits suicide.

What about the sex? I hear you ask.

It was good.

There was something aloof about Eddie in general, and with every new encounter he could feel himself removing brick after brick in her wall of remoteness. And as the emotions were released, the embraces became tighter and all-consuming, born of sheer desperation, hemmed in by the obligatory time restrictions that bound the two of them.

And as the love grew stronger, the emotions moved ever more out of control.

Although she would never say so, he felt that she always wanted the fucking to be harder, more violent. It wasn't his style, but there were moments when, moving in and out of her, his hands would involuntarily rise towards her throat and hold her tighter, press against her skin ever so slightly, evading the mad temptation to squeeze. And Eddie would gasp and gaze at him with that unfathomable look in her sad eyes.

She was one of the few women he had ever been with who would keep her eyes open during the love-making, drinking it all in, scrutinising the spasms of pain and pleasure in his face. At first he found this somewhat unsettling, but he grew to like it and wouldn't have swapped the intensity of the experience for anything in the world.

Shards.

The way she would gently wet her fingers with saliva before taking his penis in her hand and later her mouth.

The uncontrollable waves of pleasure that coursed through her like electricity when he touched her wet arsehole and timidly inserted a finger there, afraid of scratching her, harming her as he distended her reluctant opening and his mind wandered over pornographic and illegal horizons of buggery.

This evening she was still having her period and she agreed to remove her tampon. They made love on the dark carpet, joined by the blood, and later had to rush out to a night chemist to purchase some cleaning material to erase the stain from the office floor.

The shocking intimacy the first time he penetrated her mouth with his tongue.

The time she burst out in uncontrollable giggles when he licked between her toes.

Radiant Eddie.

Criminal Scenario Seven

Finally, they overcome the guilt and flee their respective marriages. They find a small flat in a part of London neither of them really knows well. For a couple of months things go swimmingly, as they overdose on the joy of whole nights together, love in the morning when the sun rises and on weekend afternoons on the sofa with Italian soccer on television. Financial matters are complicated: extracting themselves from previous commitments, house payments and attempting to do the right thing vis-à-vis their previous partners, without resort to greedy lawyers. The pressures soon grow. He picks his nose in bed. She is a bit of a slob when it comes to housework and refuses to iron his shirts. The season of quarrels is soon with them, aggravated by the inner knowledge that they have burned their bridges and there is no going back. One day, when one of them returns home late with a flimsy explanation, the other jealously suspects the worst: isn't this how their own story began? Once you've betrayed a spouse, surely the second time is easier. After the ugly words, they come to blows. A head falls violently against the table corner and one of them dies.

A grey Chelsea morning. Lingering pain in his heart for what is missing. Downstairs in the corridor, the doorbell rings insistently.

'Coming, coming,' he shouts.

Slightly out of breath, he opens the door.

Two young men in bad haircuts and grey trench coats stand there with menacing looks on their faces. 'I'm sorry to disturb you, sir. We're police officers. I'm afraid we have some rather serious questions to ask. I must advise you that anything you say may be taken in evidence. Can we come in?' the shorter one moves forward through the door and past him.

'Are you acquainted with a Mrs Edwina Cambridge?' the second police office asks, following the first one in.

'Yes, I am,' he replies. What else could he say?

This Is Not A Story

Words are not enough.

Their treacherous magic can never recapture the past. Words, empowered by longing and emotion; invested with all the despair of days running out, time flowing away on its merry march; coloured with all the complexions of flesh, rotting away, aching, bursting with feelings so extreme they could kill, or at least maim, mark her soul with indelible scars.

Never enough.

Or strong enough to drain the warm blood from his body and transfuse it to a cold, unfeeling heart.

Words are bankrupt.

This writer's words won't change the world, or even one single person's sad destiny. Throw them all away. The long ones, the short ones, a bit like cocks. Flush all the jumbled letters down the toilet, the fat ones and the thin ones alike, just like the highlights, once adored, of a woman's anatomy. No more words. Useless. Tall ones, curly ones, brown-eyed ones, the cunt-shaped ones. Words that smell of alien breath, white skin and scarlet lips.

All fucking useless now, he realises.

Remembers the tale of the monkeys who could rewrite Shakespeare given the time and the million-to-one coincidences (albeit on a manual typewriter — unlike him, the proverbial monkeys haven't recently switched to an already obsolete word processor).

Sniggers: isn't this the way he assembles his books? Lines up one word after another and then yet more until they make some sort of sense to him, but little sense to most of the others who really count. Words, lines, paragraphs.

Shit!

Should have been a musician. Taken those piano lessons. Bought that Bert Weedon how-to-play-guitar manual back when the Shadows made the instrument deadly fashionable (come to think of it, he used to wear square, dark-framed glasses like Hank Marvin and also had exaggerated sideburns down his gaunt cheeks).

And now he'd be seeking balconies all over London to serenade the bountiful, beautiful girls of summer. A bit noisy, he supposes, but surely more effective than jerking away at a keyboard.

He thinks of the right songs to sing. Songs of conquest. Tunes of triumphant romanticism to woo the pretty straw-haired blondes, the impish redheads with freckles absolutely all over, the dark, dangerous brunettes. Hear these songs, this hit parade to make your heart melt, to steal you away from unworthy husbands or boorish boyfriends, even Eurasian girlfriends. *Anchor Me* by the Mutton Birds. *Runaway Wind* by Paul Westerberg. *Shake* by the Vulgar Boatmen. Almost anything by Counting Crows, Sam Phillips, his old flame Bridget St John, Leonard Cohen, Aimee Mann, John Martyn or the Walkabouts. Then thinks the better of it; Nick Hornby's done it already.

So, pragmatically, back to all the words.

The words which say nothing. Mean everything.

Begins a story of sorts.

Paris in the 1960s. Françoise Hardy, Jacques Dutronc, Hughes Auf ray singing Dylan, Brel is dead but add him to the soundtrack anyway. A party in a rather squalid flat on the rue St Denis shared by two friends. One is French, the other English. The drink flows, the stains on the linoleum floor grow ever darker as a cocktail of liquids spills over the course of the evening. One is merry, the other glum. This girl he lusts for has not come, or maybe she did and left early with another. At any rate, he sulks. An uninvited guest tells him about this other party on Sunday. Why doesn't he come along? He notes the address. Never thinking of going. Something, the weather, his mood, changes on Sunday and he seeks out the apartment in the 16th *arrondissement*. Much of the usual crowd, junior bankers, bores, guys from the consulate. Downs a few drinks to kill time, planning an early exit. Two young women walk in. The brunette is dazzling. He only has eyes for her. He waits for the record to change, something slow, something he can talk over and be understood. He walks over to invite her to the dance floor. But some jerk moves in front of him, and like a fool he's standing face to face with the dark-haired girl's friend, a blonde. She smiles. Accepts the invite. Dances with him. One tune. Then another. Jenny and her only arrived in Paris earlier in the week. They have short-term secretarial contracts at the OECD. She's nice. Jenny, the brunette, is still deep in conversation with bloody Roland Thompson. Her name is Lois. They keep on talking. She's from South London. Blackheath or Greenwich, he can't hear properly. Suggests a walk. All the way to Chatelet by the river bank. Paris, the Seine, he doesn't know what, but the magic works on her like a spell in a book, the lights around the Concorde, the trees towering over the Ile de la Cité. He invites her up for a drink. She accepts. They fumble, embrace in the dark. The flat still smells of stale alcohol and cigarettes from the previous evening's party. He touches her breasts. They fuck. Clumsily. In the morning, she is in no mood to rush back to her temporary hotel room. They go to the Halles for breakfast. Go back to the flat (his French flatmate is visiting relatives), fuck again. Her name is Lois. She stays for weeks. He meets her friend Jenny, the brunette who initially made him think of Gina Lollobrigida. She has spots and actually looks rather plain in the open daylight. Lois is his first real love affair. She has long straight hair like Julie Christie and a small scar on her chin. One day, he reads her diary and discovers she finds him exotic. Also learns about all her earlier lovers in excruciating detail. He finds her beautiful. Loves to see her wearing his shirts and guide him gently into her, a woman of experience. One day, it's lasted almost four months, she of course breaks away. He takes a razor to his wrists. Badly. Has to return to London in disgrace.

Discards the story. Too commonplace. Ordinary. '60s kitchen sink.

He remembers once stealing a glance at another woman, another lover's diary. They were staying at a hotel in Amsterdam, great view over the canals. She had gone out for some mineral water. She had written that he had a big cock, huge dark balls and that his come had tasted acid on her tongue.

Yes, that's more like it. Make it dirty. Make the reader hard, or wet. Stories should consist of more than just words. Emotions. Images of beauty. Blood. Secretions.

Starts again.

This time, it begins with a man thinking of topless beaches under a Southern sun. He imagines breasts in all shapes and colours and sizes. He walks out of his marriage by going out for cigarettes at the corner store, leaving wife and screaming kids behind for good. A motorway ride, neon motels, vast publicity hoardings and a few nights later, he reaches the coast. It's winter. The resort is almost empty. The water laps silently against the grey sandy shore. Finds a hotel with rococo architecture and settles in for the after season. All sorts of strange people inhabit the hotel, clowns, shamans, engineers, haiku sculptors, acrobats, rock stars who have lost their magic, women. They all mingle, they mix, socialise, talk, argue, they drink into the early hours, couples form, fuck, separate, reassemble in different combinations. Regardless of whose room it might happen to be, bodies shine pale in the darkness of night, flesh against flesh, juices mingling, tongues on cunts, fingers lingering, mouths on cocks, limbs akimbo between soiled sheets, private parts rubbing frenetically against each other, hearts beating wildly while the waves of pleasure rise, souls reaching for... beyond, something more, some raging scream within all of them seeking release. He meets her, once again she is blonde. They mate with the fury of animals. But the following week, she shares her bed, her favours with other men already. His heart is broken. He listens to her moans, the frenzied rise of her lust through the wafer-thin hotel wall that separates their respective rooms as yet another violates her, possesses her, enters her, marks her indelibly both within and outside. He finds out about the conspiracy. The plot. Why all of them are here, journeyed to this forgotten hotel from all corners of the continent. They are explorers; seekers for the other side. The country that is death. And the mechanical lovemaking is not just an expression of their unbridled passions. It is the way they hope to break on through. Orgasm. *La petite mort*. Fucking themselves to death to attain the dubious immortality of the world beyond. He retreats from their frantic activities of the flesh. Of course, he is also jealous, envious, feels rejected like never before. One morning, he walks over to her room. He needs to talk. Empty. Crumpled sheets, stained with the fruit of so many nightly emissions, clothes strewn far and wide, a shoe, a garter belt, a lone nylon stocking, her black bustier, her soft contact lens case. But she is gone. He tries all the other rooms in the hotel. They have all disappeared. Crossed the frontier and reached the other side of death. Which he imagines is a country shaped like the naked body of a woman, a giantess spread-eagled in the sand. He is the only one left. The one who remains alive, left behind by the expeditionary force. He walks down to the shore. Faces the sea. Screams out his pain. Knowing that there is now nothing he can do, or say, or write, that will bring her back. Buries his head in the incoming waves, even though he knows this is the incorrect way to commit suicide.

Wrong, all wrong. He's not writing fucking science fiction any more!

Realism, lad. Realism. Isn't that what he was preaching at the crime writers' conference?

One more go, then.

Now, it starts in Miami. Moon high up in the sky, golden beach, horizon of skyscrapers, quaintness of the Art Deco District and all that. This blonde, English of course, down on her luck, scraping a living on the edges of illegality, stripping in local burlesques, a bit of lap dancing on the side in seedy joints off Collins Avenue. Meets a guy. A drug deal. South American connection. Good stuff. Hasn't got enough cash for the initial down payment so she lets the creep fuck her in the arse. That's the guy's fantasy. It's more painful than she ever thought. And he keeps on coming back for more. Finally, the stuff is shipped in and she's delegated to baby-sit the consignment for a week until the heat surrounding the main men dissipates. She bolts pronto. Keeps it all. Does a deal with this other chap who works at the film studios and always wants her to take part in fuck films. He doesn't even get her a very good price for the dope. But for her, it's enough to escape. She buys a car and flees North on the crazy American highways. *Road to Nowhere* by Talking Heads. The drug people send an enforcer after her. It becomes a wild chase, veering from state to state as they keep on missing each other. She beds all sorts of wrong men on the way. One of them somehow guesses the trouble she's in and takes off after her, romantic, smitten, hoping to shield her from the dark forces looming, to protect her. The enforcer kills the wrong woman by mistake in Austin. Now there are three of them on the road. The blonde, the romantic kid and the killer. They cross paths, separate, collide, always on the run in their private road movie. She is caught and, in a motel room in New Mexico, the thug tortures her, scars her cheek, extinguishes his cigar on her breasts, for the sadistic sake of it. She is rescued by the younger man and they now flee together. Always North. Now, the bad guy is really furious. Next time, he swears, he will kill her long before he mutilates her. This, he knows, he is going to enjoy. At night, always sleeping in his car, he dreams of the way his knife will slice through her white flesh and the mementos he will keep of her and the ways he will defile what is left of her body. He jerks off all over the front of his pale brown chinos. San Francisco. She initiates the younger guy into mild forms of bondage before they fuck, but leaves him tied up in the morning and escapes alone in the direction of Seattle. Here, by Puget Sound, in the deserted old docks area, matters come to a climax and all three protagonists finally converge for one last, tragic encounter. Shots.

Blood. It ends with her begging her younger lover standing there with tears running down his cheeks to kill her, get it over with. She no longer has any reason to live for. He obeys her.

But it's all letters, words, sentences, stories. Ain't it?

Pointless.

Not a single word can approximate the tenderness of one hand touching another. Or a pair of gently dark myopic eyes interrogating the open space separating one man and one woman. Or the quality of silence when everything has been said. Or the architecture of absence.

Wrong words. Right words. Words always in the wrong order.

This is not a story.

This is only one man's life.

Ceci n'est pas une histoire vraie.

Kate's Cunt

A Story of Pornography and Longing

See, I wanted to tell you about Kate's cunt.

Maybe I'm growing older less gracefully than I thought, growing older badly. But so often these days, my memory plays tricks on me, the object of my search eludes me and I struggle for the right images, shapes and colours. For several weeks after our first meeting, I just could not recall the colour of her eyes. Brown, of course, as I found out the next time, the time, the first, she allowed me to unveil her breasts.

It's been a couple of years now, and not a single day has gone by when I haven't thought of her with ever- agonising longing. I scream in my sleep, I cry inside while I amble down familiar streets and cities, praying for the day she no longer intrudes and I can set the whole episode away for good. But no, every little thing reminds me of her. A poster, a newspaper headline, the way another woman walks, dresses, styles her hair, and memories of Kate flood back like a torrent, washing back the pain in their wake.

Visions of her body, her whiteness, her voice, the way she said on that final occasion: 'I've never hated anyone in my life as much as I hate you'.

Yes, I remember it all. The good things, the bad things, the silly, irrelevant things. All. But somehow, even with this killing cast-iron memory of mine, I can't recall her cunt.

Kate's cunt.

The geography, the anatomy, the folds, the ridges, the textures, the tactile feel of its landscape as my fingers, my tongue, my soul ranged over, across and inside it and I could hear her moans, her sighs, the pleasure coursing through her body almost like a million miles away.

Kate's cunt.

The many colours, moving from pink to red to brown and all the myriad shades in between, a racing one-tone rainbow from outer lips to inner lips, clit hood, vaginal walls, the wondrous, shocking intimacy of her radiant innards.

Kate's cunt.

Its wetness and smell engulfing my cock, its taste flirting with the sensors of my tongue, the sponge-like humidity leaking over my lips and under my nails.

But aren't these all just words, the vocabulary of sex, clichés that come too easily to my finger tips as I type these sad evocations of tousle-haired Kate?

Are words now my only allies in recalling the truth about her cunt? But they mean so little now, as my mind struggles to remember that small part of her and I fail abysmally, I guess. I almost remember every beauty spot, mole or imperfection dotted across the vast landscape of her body, every modulation of her smile and the way she laughed when I cracked a bad joke or uttered stupid endearments. The pauses in our telephone conversations, the food we ate, almost always ethnic, the individual benches or chairs we sat on in pubs and hotel bars. Oh, I could weave a boring symphony of lust requited about the time we spent together, the number of times we coupled, the surfaces we fucked on, whether floor, carpet tiles, desks, beds, bathrooms in and out of slippery tubs, rickety cheap sofas, wet grass in parks with goosebumps spreading across our flesh. I could switch into pornographic mode and enumerate all the variations and positions we manoeuvred our compliant bodies into to copulate, to make the pleasure last, stronger, more intense, her long legs held up over my shoulders as I dug my cock ever deeper into her, feeling like an assassin of love, spearing her insides, reaching almost her heart with the engorged circumcised tip of my ugly purplish cock and she would cry 'Jesus, Jesus' as patches of orgasmic flush spread across her neck and shoulders. Yes, I remember all that and the lost feeling in my heart that kept growing stronger with every word and encounter. Indeed. But as I dredge up all the memories, I still cannot recall her wonderful cunt, the anatomical essence of my Kate, my past lover and it hurts me like bloody hell, because if I cannot tell you about Kate's cunt, then in a crazy way I know I am betraying her and everything we stood for. Doesn't make sense, does it? Try and bear with me, though.

Once upon a time, I know, she was a shy young girl growing up in leafy, suburban Epsom, her dark sad eyes gazing at the world with anger and frustration. Rebellious, often governed by her fierce temper, finding solace in books, always getting involved in stupid, needless rows with her parents. Already fighting for her independence. Over her teenage years, she grows wondrously tall, lanky, though she feels her hips are too large and her tits not sufficiently opulent. She becomes a woman in body, though her mind still swims in a morass of doubt and anxiety.

She strips, one morning whilst alone in the house, her mother is out doing the weekly shopping, in front of the bathroom mirror. She travels up and down the length of her body, amazed in a frightened sort of way, by the sheer whiteness of its smooth, compliant expanse, the light brown mole, there, near the tip of her left breast, the intricately sculpted crevice of her navel and the dark curls that have grown beneath it. She slips her fingers through this strange pubic tangle, an Amazon explorer making her way through the matted alien vegetation, she feels the ridge of her outer lip, shyly inserts a finger into the warmth. A curious feeling as the nail brushes against a growing wetness. She looks up at her face in the mirror. Her eyes appear -to be asking a question she has no answer for. She lowers her gaze to her genital area again. Opens her long legs a bit more, increasing the geometrical angle, the empty pyramid shape of light beneath her sex. Her eyes move again, towards the glass shelf above the wash basin. Her father's razor. He is a traditionalist, a wet shaver. The blue stem of a toothbrush, standing at attention in a plastic mug. She takes the toothbrush between her fingers, deliberately lowers it towards her cunt and slowly inserts its rounded extremity between the curls, the dark lips she knows lie behind her tangled bush. She feels little. She moves it in deeper, in a circular movement. A dangerous thought races through her fevered mind, something she has read somewhere, that blood flows freely when the hymen breaks. But her friend Julia who still insists that she did it with this boy from the nearby modern comprehensive, had told her there was no blood on that first time. Kate doesn't believe her. She gyrates the thin stalk of the toothbrush inside her and that tingling feeling returns. She can see her cheeks redden in the mirror, reminding her of the way she always blushes when she lies to her mum and ends up getting caught for whatever latest transgression she has been up to. The colour invading her pale cheeks betrays her. The small scar below her right cheek, from that old playground fight, stands out. She quickly withdraws the brush. She sighs deeply. She is sixteen. She is so fucking beautiful already, but doesn't know it, doubts it.

Again, she spies the razor. Mad thoughts race like a gale across her mind. The object is shaped like a letter T. The upright bar is black, thicker than the toothbrush. She takes hold of her father's alien implement, gingerly, daringly.

She opens the bathroom door, leaving it at an angle so that she can still see herself in the tall mirror when she moves back and sits on the toilet. She opens her legs and watches as the faint trace of her cunt lips pierce the encroaching darkness of her matted curls. She spreads her thighs wider. Moves the razor downwards. Brushes it against the damn hair. She feels wet inside, wetter than ever before, even more than when she had read that book the other month, she senses a river of confused feelings melting through her. She pulls the razor across the first clump, in a steady downward movement. The curls thin. She continues. Sometimes, the razor blade catches a stray hair and pulls it rather than cuts it. Pain. But she repeats the movement of the razor over the recalcitrant area and quickly glimpses the smoothness underneath. She doesn't know that shaving foam would make the whole thing easier. Soon, her cunt is visible in the mirror, bare, speckled with red blotches from the painful scraping, jutting from her white body almost. A defiant gate to her churning insides, a raw gash, bald, the swollen outer flesh somewhat plump like that of a new-born baby, but she continues gazing at her now-unadorned forbidden zone, tries to remember what it had looked like before the darker curls had grown. And realises that her cunt is now different, aged, ready. For what, she briefly wonders? Her heart knows. She drops the razor to the tiled bathroom floor and inserts a finger, then another one inside and closes her eyes. Her dead teenage curls float listlessly on the undisturbed surface of the toilet bowl under her square arse and her now-inflamed cunt.

This was a day long ago. I don't know what I must have been doing right then. Marvelling at the way the clouds floated across a mountain valley behind my hotel window in the Italian Alps or stumbling through the undergrowth in the furrows of a banana plantation in Panama. I didn't know her then.

Of course, I was already so much older than her and would have laughed if someone had told me then that in twelve years or so I would be painfully besotted with a schoolgirl. But between then and now, her and me, there were still to be four other men, including a husband.

And she would learn to masturbate more effectively.

My own early adventures in masturbation now feel so ridiculous. I was a late, bad learner.

We lived in Paris, where in nursery school I was once beaten up by other kids, French kids, when they learned I was English and emotionally accused me of having burned Joan of Arc. Thus I first came fist to face with the sins of the past. Have I ever seen the end of them? During school holidays I was packed back to my aunt's in London where I would while away the time eating indecent amounts of chocolate, seeing every film at the local ABC, where the double features changed twice a week and hunted for second-hand copies of old science-fiction magazines and paperbacks in a dusty, shady-looking store that lurked between two furniture warehouses on Walthamstow High Street. As I grew older, I began exploring the darker depths of the store and came across a shelf of nudist publications, when the female genital areas were still completely airbrushed out. I was much more interested in my sci-fi and the then glittering career of Manchester United's Busby babes, but these curious anatomical displays had a bizarre air of fascination and I bought one of the pocket-sized magazines. Was I twelve or thirteen or older? Difficult to place the time with any amount of historical precision.

That evening in bed, after greedily consuming my latest batch of space adventures, I began perusing the black and white pages of what I realised was a 'dirty' magazine, moving between the scenes of beach volley ball where the women's breasts were distinctly larger than the ball in play, and a bevy of curiously unnatural pauses where the blank space of the model's pubes held a deep and unfathomable mystery. After much wonderment, I hid the magazine between the mattress and the bedsprings, where no doubt every generation of troubled adolescents still conceal their unauthorised educational material. That night I woke up for the first time with an erection. It was a strange feeling, both frightening — what is this happening to my body? and gently pleasurable. I watched this seemingly huge cock I had grown in my sleep with sheer awe. Sometimes touching it, to feel a surge of electric current racing through me that scared me even more. Eventually, the alien cock subsided, leaving a million unanswered questions coursing through my grey cells. I went to pee, reassured it was still functioning properly, and finally managed to fall asleep again. Soon, the strange adventure of my living penis began occurring almost every night. My deductive powers finally blamed the curious recurring event of my cock coming to life to the fact that I slept on my stomach and that somehow the friction of my penis against the bedsheet was responsible for the incident. I even began to look forward to the weird event in a perverse way; it never dawned on me that this might happen to other boys. I thought I had become a bit of a freak, and was rather proud of it!

When I returned to Paris and my family, the phenomenon of the growth became more infrequent. I mused on the implications: was it the water? the air? the food? or was my illness finally fading away? If so, I was going to miss it; it had quickly become one of the main events of my limited secret social life.

Friction, hey?

Could I create 'the rise' by artificial means? I could try. The possibility of simply using my hands never arose.

So, after a rather ridiculous process of trial and error experimentation with the limited amount of likely implements available in a typical middle-class Paris two-room apartment, I finally perfected my ideal erection method. Whenever my parents would go out at night (and frantically on Saturday mornings, in their perilously short and unpredictable shopping period, but by then, I was hooked, and the desperate need for a quick erection and now the wondrous release of newly-found ejaculations, rejected all notion of danger), I would go at it with feverish rage.

First, I would strip and run around the flat naked to the door that separated the living room from the small kitchen. Here, I would place a stool against the door, step on it and grip the top of the door, then kick the stool away. This left me hanging bare-arse naked from the door, cock squashed against the smooth, light-brown surface of the painted wood. Any onlooker would have died laughing. Then came the traction, all the muscles in my arms pulling my puny body up and creating the necessary pressure and friction against my dangling cock until it grew hard and I would manage to spray the door with my ejaculate, before my arms gave up in utter exhaustion. Ah, the rue Laurence Savart kitchen door! I knew it well. Receptacle a hundred times over of my innocent come, my first wasted seed. The door my mother never wondered about, always immaculately clean, from my instant damage limitation. Come is as good as soap, you know. Its splashes pearling down the door in several bifurcating streams, which I would always catch and mop up before they reached the ground. Did my mother ever suspect? Maybe she did.

The door of a hundred orgasms. Sounds like the title of a pulp novelette. This was also the time when I discovered the horror stories of HP Lovecraft. It was, I think, almost a year before Georges, my best friend, whom I finally confided my terrible secret to, taught me that what I had been doing so clumsily actually had a name and could be achieved so much easier manually and with the assistance of visual aids.

Today, I no longer need nudist magazines, even though they have graduated beyond the art of airbrushing genitals. All I do is think of Kate's cunt.

See how I come.

Like in a bad porno movie, my ejaculate bursts free from the top of my cock, and rains down on her raised backside. We're in a motel outside Phoenix, Arizona. It's warm for February. I look down at her body, the moon- shaped twin hemispheres of her white, smooth arse, my eyes fixed on the dilated anal aperture whence I extricated my member. I smell our sweat, a pungent aroma, invisible streams blending in the air; I wipe my cock clean with my hand and bring the fingers to my nose to sniff the slight fecal odour. The faint flavour of my lover's shit which I have scraped against and ploughed inside of her.

'Are you sure it didn't hurt?' I ask.

'A bit at first,' she replies. 'I really didn't think it would manage to get in that far without tearing me apart. It felt enormous. It burnt. Then, when you were finally in, maybe I was less nervous, so I relaxed, and it started feeling good. And you began to move, Jesus, I thought I was going to die, the feeling was so strong. And all I wanted was literally to be consumed by you. Eaten alive. Fucked senseless up the arse. Sodomised. The word sounds so odd.'

Back in England, we'd talked about it several times, but had never got around to attempting anal sex. She would become increasingly agitated and sensitive whenever I would slip a finger into her back hole whilst making love to her in the missionary po-

90

sition, writhing in pleasurable agony, darting her tongue into my ear, and I knew that she was attracted to the idea, but also scared. We had prepared carefully, engaging in lengthy foreplay until our senses were crying out for some form of penetration and release, before I had — memories of the movies — spread some butter around her hole and she had dipped my cock into an ocean of saliva to ease the lubrication.

I kept on gazing at the inflamed, pink skin around the hole which was now closing up again. I lowered my head and licked the humid perimeter. A shudder coursed through her body.

'Have you ever been fucked that way?' she asked me later that evening, once we were back under the white sheets.

'No, I've never had any homosexual experiences.'

'But would you like to be entered there?'

'Yeah, I'd love to know what it feels like, but the idea of a man doing it to me doesn't appeal in the slightest. If only you could grow a cock, that's how I'd want you to rape me,' I said.

'We'll get a big fat vibrator, and I'll fuck you until you scream. That's a promise.' And she quickly fell asleep, as a gentle wind from the New Mexico mountains brushed against the window pane.

The next day she had her period. Still, we fucked like crazies, painting the hotel bed with her blood, red spreading like a pattern across her thighs, my cock dipping into the boiling jam of her essence with no regard for propriety or taboos. We were mad. After the act, our spent bodies crucified across the bed, wallowing in the moist warmth, I slipped my whole hand into her cunt and scooped up my come and her congealed issue and distributed it over her breasts and my chest, rubbing the dubious mixture into the skin, anointing our lust with this unforgettable sacrament.

So, for a few days, I had to abandon my occupation of her cunt. We'd cleaned the sheets as best we could, before leaving the motel for another in the next state along our American journey.

And, night after night, she would take my hungry cock into her mouth before impaling her white arse on it, an occasional tear pooling up around her eyes when the pain became too intense. But she never asked me to stop. Never. Anyway, what we were doing was probably illegal in that particular state anyway.

The geography of Kate's arse-hole. Unlike most women, the skin around the aperture did not grow darker; it remained unnaturally pale, like the rest of her body, just turning a deep red from the intense friction when I penetrated her and the sphincter muscles rebelled against the intrusion. I also wondered how I could get in sometimes. My cock is medium in length but quite thick when totally engorged, and to enable the final thrust to break through her body's resistance and the head to move in beyond the concentric circle of her crevice, I had to hold the stem of my cock hard between my clenched fingers to force more blood towards the tip and make the cock even more rigid at the moment of anal penetration. In magazines and films, I've seen black guys with cocks not only enormous in length, but thick as giant bonsai tree trunks, and, so tell me I'm politically incorrect, I've often fantasised how women could humanly accommodate them. Especially in instances of rear entry. Particularly blondes. Yes, I do dream of Kate on a bed, servicing three black men with massive cocks, one in her mouth, one in her cunt, and one digging like a lunatic with his instrument of torture up her rear hole. This is how I torture myself when I can no longer recall the image of Kate's cunt when I jerk off, when I come in shame, when I am in pain.

As I write these infamous lines on my laptop.

Together, we travelled. Airport lounges and plastic food, badly-lit motel rooms and American highways. The first obscene road movie. Diners and giant sandwiches and diesel fumes.

In Vancouver, she fucked me with a pink flesh- coloured vibrator, purchased from a small sex shop which lurked darkly behind the harbour, nearby Gas Town. It didn't hurt, but neither did I find it pleasant or exciting. She pushed the implement in too far and too hard and tore the skin. I bled quite heavily.

In Seattle, she had her cunt lips pierced by this huge tattooed guy in an underground head shop close by the Egyptian Cinema on Capitol Hill, and I bought a gold ring which he inserted. That evening, our hotel room was on the 24th floor of the Madison Stouffer Tower, overlooking the speckled beauty of Puget Sound. Here, I shaved away the thin curls around her cunt to keep the ring unencumbered and visible. It shone in the artificial chiaroscuro of the hotel room like a diamond, highlighted by her engorged outer lips, the puffy, darkening portals of flesh guarding her vagina, the wetness from within patently leaking over their protuberance.

'Would you want me to have my nipples pierced also?' she asked.

I did not answer, hypnotised by the wonderfully indecent spectacle of her wide open thighs, her gaping shaven wound and the gold ring, that seal of joint infamy.

'Maybe I should shave all that messy hair around your cock. Could I?' she suggested. 'It would make it look so much longer.'

'Isn't it long enough? I queried.

Mischief glinted down in the depths of her dark brown eyes, and moved silently down to her scarlet, painted lips.

We coupled like animals in heat, rutting, moaning, sighing, screaming, oiling our bodies with fragrant lotions and all manners of creams and grease, explorers searching for the very limits of lust.

Missoula.

Atlanta.

Washington.

Chicago.

Finally, our genitals sore and blistered, London again. A familiar terrain. Reassuring faces and places. Fearful dangers and uncertainties.

Shortly after the return to England.

Kate felt cold. She slipped on my grey tee-shirt, the one dotted with Donald Duck figures. It fitted her to perfection. The cotton fabric like a warm second skin, the 3D silhouette of her hardened nipples jutting through the thin shirt with impudent innocence. She stood up, her tall beauty towering through the hotel room. The tee-shirt reached to just below her navel. Her sex exposed, her backside bare. She turned away from me, moving towards the bathroom. Her cunt now hidden from me. My eyes lingering in usual awe over the lunar expanse of her regal arse.

The last time I saw Kate's cunt.

Four days later, she left me.

Denied forever and eternity the widescreen vision at the heart of her inner thighs.

I remember her eyes now, the soft plastic contact lenses she would replace every week; her small, firm breasts; the perfume of the mousse she massaged into her curls at the start of the day; her lanky posture; the gap between her crooked teeth.

But, no longer, the object of my desire.

F.u.c.k.

C.u.n.t.

Four-letter words of sheer beauty.

Kate, my radiant, mixed-up Kate, I want you back.

To savour again the musky taste of your cunt. To move my tongue inside you, to spread the bruises of lust across your body, to eat your cunt, force its fragrant ramparts with my wrinkled cock, to kiss your hundred lips with my madness.

Sit on me.

Lower your cunt over my face, my mouth, my confused heart.

Ah, to see Kate's cunt again.

Just Like A James M Cain Story, Only Cheaper

Casey slept in the window seat.
Flight AA3O crept over the Atlantic, inching its way high above the coast of Newfoundland.

Plane journeys from Europe to the West Coast just go on forever.

As Casey dozed, Jake could not help himself endlessly staring at her.

'Why are you so fucking beautiful?' he asked her silently. 'Christ, why do I love her so much that words can no longer suffice?' he wondered, drinking in her features with utter greed. The sky outside the plane formed a perfect backdrop for the sheer delicacy of her features. The blue heavens passed slowly by, marbled with streaks of white cloud, as the Boeing-seven-whatever made its interminable way from London to Los Angeles.

Boisterous, bored kids ran up and down the aisles, neglected by parents and attendants. Some cried. Other passengers queued impatiently for the toilets. The first movie had finished some fifteen minutes before. He didn't know if there was to be a second. He could never watch films on planes; the screens were to small, the distractions around too many, and he was aware that they screened cut, abridged versions anyway. Her face in sleep was so innocent. Casey, my second life, he reflected, watching the quiet movement of her chest, as her breath ebbed in and out of her blanket-covered body. The stewardess stopped by.

'Another coffee, sir?'

He emerged from his daydream to acknowledge her and ordered a soft drink instead.

'Without ice, please.'

Casey slept on.

So, this was it. Now she was finally his; although, if confronted with such an assertion, she would certainly have reacted angrily that she belonged to no one. They were together at last. Somehow, he still couldn't believe it: he had managed, by hook or by crook, by lies, half truths and deception, seduction, guile and subtle moral blackmail cum manipulation, to tear her away from that fool of a husband.

A ray of blinding light shone through the cabin window, losing itself in the curling jungle of her blonde hair and Jake held his breath. His heart almost faltered. It should be illegal to be so damn beautiful! Mine. With me. Here. On the way to the States, which she had never visited before.

Impossible.

This could not be, this was a parallel life, like in a science fiction story. In real life, he was still heartbroken, aching in his guts at the thought of Casey still sleeping in the marital bed with that other man who mounted her without grace, poetry or even talent. In the actual world, as opposed to the virtual realm of his wish fulfilment, she now refused to see him any longer, hated his guts with a vengeance and would no longer even answer his letters full of rage, self-pity and desperation.

He turned again. She still slept, her pale face impassive. On their return, she had agreed, they would move in together somewhere, some flat they would find, she already had put all her belongings in storage, and they would instigate the necessary legal paperwork to sunder the final ties with their earlier incarnations. It would be messy, costly, sometimes heartbreaking, but it would happen.

A thought occurred: maybe they wouldn't even go back to England?

A needless announcement over the plane's Tannoy system.

Casey lazily opened her eyes.

Saw Jake pensively staring at her.

'What are you looking at me like that?' she asked.

'Dunno. Maybe thinking I don't deserve this luck,' he answered.

'Well, maybe you don't,' she said, stirring upwards in her seat, readjusting the crooked airline stance of her long legs. 'Please, Jake, don't keep on looking at me like that. Makes you look bovine.'

Their stewardess ambled down the aisle and brought them hot towels. Then Casey got up to visit the toilet, to readjust her make-up. For a brief moment, Jake toyed with the idea of suggesting he join her there. He'd never done it on a plane. Mile High Club and all that. But he didn't. Casey appeared to be in a funny mood.

The seat-belt warning light came on followed by an announcement of turbulence.

He began reading a boring article in the in-flight magazine on why Norwegians had elected by referendum not to join the EEC.

'Oh, Jake, please, don't do that.'

'Do what?'

'Picking your nose.'

'Sorry, I didn't even realise I was.'

'It's really disgusting.'

'Sorry, I'll try. When I'm reading, watching a movie, sort of not aware of it, you know.'

'Well, you'll really have to try better in future, if we are to live together.'

'I thought we were living together, Casey.'

'All the more so, then.'

'Casey, you're so unforgiving of other people's weaknesses, aren't you?'

'So what?'

'I remember that time in Brighton at the hotel, during our first week-end together, you telling me about that boyfriend you moved in with at University and how from the first morning you knew it wasn't going to last, because the poor sod wet shaved and left the ensuing mess in the sink. Didn't give him a chance, did you?'

'No.'

'But you gave your husband seven years of chances, though, didn't you? Including all those bloody months when I was already around and begging you to leave him, hey?'

'Jake, I don't want to talk about my husband. Understood? You've hurt him enough as it is.'

'We've hurt him, you mean?'

'You. Me. What difference does it make?'

'You're right. We have to put the past behind us. Completely.'

'And do I ever ask you about your wife, your children? Do I?

'Point taken, Casey. Behind us. It's just now that counts.'

'So keep your fucking fingers out of your fucking big nose, Jake. And by the way, what are we doing today?'

'I thought I'd get some work done on the laptop. Get a bit further ahead on that story I'd promised the magazine. The deadline is coming up.'

'What about me?'

'Didn't you want to go to Santa Monica to get the new Springsteen CD. The semi-acoustic one; that song on the radio was so good.'

'Will you drive me there?'

'Sure, and I'll pick you up later. You know, Casey, you really should learn to drive.'

'Why? So I should be out of your way when you want to work?'

'No, that's not what I meant. You'd be more independent. Able to do things without having to rely on me so much.'

'I know. I have to, the sun, the beach, it's all a bit much at times. I've got to do something about my life here. I have aspirations.'

'So you say.'

'My husband was so ambitious, it ruled his life. Used to berate me for not having ambitions. But I did. Just didn't know what they were.'

'You just said you didn't want to talk about your husband, Casey.'

'Oh fuck you, I'll talk about what I want to. Can't remember us having many scintillating conversations of late, once you discount books, films and music, can I?'

'That's not fair. Remember the times when you said that our silences were worth a thousand words. That we were at our closest when we were together in silence?'

'Well, we weren't living together then, were we?'

Baggage recovered, past the automatic doors into the outside heat.

'Jesus, it's so warm. Look, palm trees!' said Casey, eyes wide with wonder.

'Welcome to California, my love,' Jake said. 'Wait until I take you to Las Vegas one day. There, they have slot machines in the airport concourses. Hits you as soon as you de-plane, as they say here. This is the New World.'

'Funny place, America,' Casey remarked, pushing the luggage trolley toward the car hire pick-up area, while Jake struggled forward, balancing further bags and his computer case from straps continuously slipping from his shoulders.

While waiting for the courtesy coach, watching the large cars and sundry hotel and car hire vehicles whiz by on the LAX circular feed road, Jake and Casey fell into another long silence. Jet lag? In London it was now night and dark. An awkward realisation that all the bridges to the past were now well burned, nay incinerated?

'For the rest of our lives,' Jake said, deliberately interrupting the uneasy peace.

Casey looked back at him, the sun creating a golden halo behind her head.

Jake smiled.

She didn't.

'Maybe,' she answered, gravely.

Half an hour queuing in the concrete pavilion of the car hire company, jostling with a phalanx of incoming tourists, voices in Spanish and German mostly, some French and the occasional Scandinavian.

'I hate it,' said Jake. 'All the rental cars are automatic. I prefer manual. Habit, I suppose.'

'It's not a very big car,' Casey remarked after they had stuffed all their luggage in the trunk and on the back seat.

'When we've found a place to stay,' Jake answered, 'we'll buy one. You can choose the colour.'

'Yeah.'

'How good are you at navigating?' Underlining their route to the coast on the map.

'Hopeless, I warn you,' she replied.

'Doesn't matter. Even if we stray, we'll end up at the sea. Can't miss it.'

They drove out of the rental compound, Jake still instinctively wanting to put both feet down on the pedals and trying to remember how to drive on the right hand side of the road as the sluggish Chevy Cavalier moved over the security bumps and the attendant checked his papers.

'Right here, all the way to Airport Boulevard,' Casey instructed.

He moved hesitantly into the traffic.

He soon had the hang of it again and they cruised back toward LAX to the intersection with the highway that would lead them to the coastal resorts.

'Look, Jake. That's so funny!' They were waiting at a set of lights. Casey pointed at a large, oval-shaped building by the roadside. Outside the shuttered place, there was a tall sign which identified the joint as a strip club. It also advertised, in red wonky plastic letters:

Female Dancers Very Wanted.

'Smacks of desperation if you ask me,' Jake said, as the lights finally turned green and he drove off. 'They're ready to take anybody on, as long as she has tits and a round arse.'

'I've never seen a real strip tease act,' Casey said to him. 'There were a couple of times when the sales people asked me to join them in Frankfurt but I never wanted to go. Seen some in movies, but I'm sure it's not the same thing. Have you ever been to one, Jake?'

'Yes. A long time ago. I gather they're much more explicit these days, particularly here.'

'I'd love to see one. Will you take me?'

'Sure, if you find it that interesting,' Jake replied.

Casey moved her hand toward him and stroked his thigh.

'Maybe they'd even give me a job, if we end up in dire need of money.'

Jake chuckled. She sure could still surprise him. The highway sign appeared. This is where he had to turn off.

Halfway there, they drove by another roadside place, this one with less architectural ambition, more like a Mexican stone shack with gaudy garlands of red lights surrounding its door and grilled windows. Porno theatre. Free entrance for Ladies on Thursday night. Mixed couples live show, it advertised.

'Is a live show where they fuck on stage?' asked Casey.

'Yes.'

'And mixed couples, does it mean just a man and a woman, or do they have to have different colour skin?'

'I really don't know. You seem unusually fascinated by the more lurid side of America, Casey,' he remarked.

'Well, I have to,' she giggled, making his heart melt. 'After all, I'm a wanton woman, now. Aren't I? Jake, will you take me to a porno theatre?'

'I don't know,' he replied. 'I don't want it to give you ideas.'

'Have you ever been to a live show? Come on, tell me. After all, you've written porn.'

'Once, it was in the red light district in Amsterdam. A proper little theatre with a bogus show which ended up with this guy in a gorilla suit pulling his cock out and screwing this girl dressed up as Little Red Riding Hood on stage. But I was in the back rows and couldn't really see much.'

'Cool.'

As they neared the Pacific shore, Jake didn't know what to think of Casey's observations and questions. He could see how little he really knew her and didn't know whether this conversation excited or worried him. They left the highway at Lincoln Boulevard and drove to Marina del Rey where he had made a booking in a bed and breakfast hotel for their first week here.

In the inn's car park, he finally said to her, as he pulled the car keys out of the ignition:

'You amaze me, you know. It's your first time in America and all you see as we re driving along are the strip clubs and the porno places. What sort of dirty mind have you been hiding from me?'

'What the hell are you doing?

'Reading. What does it look that I'm doing?'

'With those tweezers, Jake?'

'Oh, that. Just pulling some unwanted hairs from my ear lobes. I hate them. Shortish, dark, feels sort of unshaven.'

'Welcome to the Disgusting World of Jake, Part 102.'

'Yes, I suppose so. I've only been doing it for a couple of years, now. Just started, those hairs sprouting in my ear as I grew older just annoyed me, you know?'

'God, this is what I'm living with. A man who plucks his ears. Anything else you pluck while I'm looking the other way? I don't think I can face any more vile bad habits.'

'Not that I can think of.'

'Absolutely sure?'

'Yes, Casey.'

'What about all those times after we fuck, when you start scratching your scalp?'

'I've told you before. After making love, it often feels so hot, irritable. My version of orgasmic flush, I suppose. Surely you understand that. It's biological. Probably means the sex was good.'

'For who?'

'Oh, come on, Casey. That's not fair. Anyway, what's up with you tonight, why do you have to pick on me? Something I've said or done or not done?'

'You get on my fucking nerves sometimes, Jake, you just do. And I'm not invoking PMT or my period as an excuse.'

'Thanks.'

'Is that all you can say in response?'

'Maybe it's this place. Too small, doesn't provide you with enough space of your own. If I can sell the book, maybe we can then afford a house, rather than an apartment.'

'I sure want to believe you, Jake.'

They fucked. They screwed. They bonked. As if there were no more tomorrow. At last, with complete impunity. No more lies, excuses, temporary hotel rooms, late meeting pretexts, sales conferences, contracts seminars.

Lust became just another word for love.

They toured the coastal realtors' offices and were shown around dozens of properties. Both Jake and Casey fell in love at first sight with the Venice Canals and their quaint waterside houses, bridges and wild plants and flowers galore, but the budget wouldn't stretch. They settled for an apartment on the sea front, between Santa Monica and Marina del Rey, with a view of the quiet, rumbling ocean and a thousand daily skateboarders and joggers buzzing by throughout the day. It wasn't perfect, but it would do. Exchanged the rental car for a small Japanese saloon. The choice was limited, but Casey went for dark brown. The colour of her eyes, Jake knew.

Life then appeared to him like an endless tomorrow of open possibilities, a million hours free to spend with her, touch her, watch her. He felt he no longer needed anything else.

First American fuck: in the dark room at the inn, the window to the balcony partly open, to appease the heat, sweaty, anxious, fumbling, unsatisfying, the thrusting and the grasping somehow full of anger and resentment. Jake came too fast. Casey, spread-eagled on the hotel regulation light brown cotton cover, a scornful look in her eye. Below them, the elevated patio where breakfast was usually served when the weather permitted.

Second American fuck. By now they had moved to the second floor flat overlooking the seafront promenade. Better. Rewarding. Palpitating with raw emotion. Outside the balcony, the Saturday night crowd, boisterous, rowdy in a joyful way, moved along. They made love right by the window, almost where people could see them. Jake carried Casey there, putting further strain on his bad back, determined to do the romantic thing. Crossing some symbolic threshold.

'Yes, by the balcony, where people can hear us,' suggested Casey.

She still wore her favourite black garter belt and stockings like the Heathrow adulteress she had once been. He slowly pulled her dress up, over her hips, baring her flat midriff, then past her shoulders. Matching black lace underwear. He freed her pale breasts and kissed her there, watching from the corner of his eyes as the pale areolae turned darker. Then removed her thin knickers. Her curly thatch speared by the revealed pinkness of her wet lower lips. They touched. His mouth, her body. Her lips, his skin. Moved in and out of complex geometrical configurations and absurd positions to heighten and sustain the angle of desire and the rise of their pleasure. Their flesh blended. Perspiration dropped from her forehead onto his chest. His scalp itched. She took him in her hand and guided him into her, clenched him inside, her thighs like a vice around his waist and adjusted her position on the cool wooden floor of the rented apartment to deepen his reach and the crazy friction between their parts. Jake watched her take her pleasure with his usual fascination, her eyes wide open, her tongue manically running to and fro across her lips to keep them moist, whenever he relaxed his kisses to momentarily catch his breath.

When she came, she screamed like a banshee in heat. She had never been that vocal back in England, in the clandestine days of their relationship. Her sounds drowned amongst the distant din of Muscle Beach, but a black guy on roller skates passing by heard her, and looked up, bemused, toward their window. Only saw their heads bobbing inside, just beyond the balcony. Somehow understood the situation and guffawed away as his wheels kept on moving.

'Quiet, Casey,' Jake pleaded. 'You'll wake up the whole neighbourhood.'

'It's wide awake already. Just the way I always thought California would be,' Casey said, her cheeks deeply flushed, catching her breath as the waves of her orgasm receded in ever so slow motion.

'It turns you on, doesn't it, that others might hear us?' Jake remarked.

'Yeah!' Casey replied. 'Let's do it in the road.'

Later that night, no moon in the sky, they made it on the beach, way past two in the morning, in the dark shadow of Venice Pier. It was cold and their intertwined bodies formed a landscape of goosebumps, a lunar sight to behold. Sand got everywhere. Back at the flat, Jake tongued her deeply, sucking out the fine grains of sand from all her orifices and hidden cavities, kneeling in the shower as she shampooed his hair.

Afterwards, as he dried her, taking advantage of the situation to touch all her vulnerable, sensitive spots further through the fluffy white towel, Jake said: 'I love you so much.'

'I know,' Casey said, with a kindness that tore his heart open even more.

He held her tight against him, pulled the towel away from her body and tripped her gently into the still warm water of the bath tub and entered her once again. Wet, squelchy underwater sex, their two back beast constricted by the walls of the tub, water splashing wildly out onto the tiles. Still inside her, he pulled her up, and they hopped, dripping, toward the bedroom, never separating, falling to the carpeted floor to rut on, every new strong thrust dislodging water and air from her innards, causing them to laugh madly at the obscene vaginal farts they were creating in their frenzy.

Over the first three weeks or so, they used every available surface of the flat to make love on, until their parts were literally raw. Except the kitchen table. Those were the good days.

'How about going to Universal City later today?'

'What for?'

'You've never been. We can leave early, get there ahead of all the crowds. Do all the main rides, the Jurassic Park one. It's supposed to be sphincter-clenching spectacular. *Back To The Future*. *ET*. *Backdraft*. *Waterworld*. The good old studio backlot tour. It'll be really great fun.'

'Come on, Jake, I had to be dragged screaming to the zoo when

I was still a kid. Hated those sort of things. And as for fun, I had enough fun back in England playing hide-the-bottle from alcoholic relatives. Aren't we a bit old for an amusement park surely? Next, you'll want to us to visit Disneyland and wear funny ears.'

'Well. There's always Citywalk, you know.'

'No. Today, I was thinking of spending some more time on the beach. Perfecting my tan. Autumn's coming. Soon, there will be less opportunities. And it's great, there's so few people out on the sand, more seagulls than humans. No carpet vendors or young punks to ogle me if I go topless.'

'My Californian beach bimbo who's always reading a book!'

'Isn't that what California is all about?'

'Yeah, I love my blonde bimbo.'

'Be careful what you say.'

'Casey?'

'Yes.'

'Oh, probably not…'

'Come on, you want to tell me something. I can see that silly romantic look in your eyes, Jake. What?'

'I was just thinking…'

'Yes? Tell me.'

'It's going to annoy you, I know. But here we go: I do so much want a child by you. A child who would look like you.'

'And why should I want one with you when I didn't want one with my husband, hey? You know how I feel about it.'

'Dunno really.'

'Don't go all broody on me, Jake. Please.'

'Okay, I won't mention the subject again; unless you bring it up first.'

'Very unlikely. But I don't think Universal City is such a good idea after all. You'll see too many cute babies there. Let's do the beach today. Your tan is much too uneven. You never lie on your stomach and the contrast between your front and back is getting pretty ridiculous. Jake, the two-tone man. And, Jake?'

'Yes?'

'You've got to do something about your weight. Those love-handles are no longer a joke. Too many of those lobsters in melted butter and garlic on Lincoln Boulevard, I fear. I'm not joking. Really.'

'You're right, Casey, I will do something about it. Promise.'

They had to go to Santa Monica. Money matters. The bank. Money was beginning to run low, the three month advance and the deposit on the rental, the car, day-to-day expenses. Jake had arranged with his accountants back in London to sell the business, but whenever that transaction was completed, half of the proceeds would go to his wife, plus the house he had volunteered to relinquish, where he had transferred his share to the children. Not guilt, he knew, but a sense of obligation. He didn't want them to grow up hating him for his desertion. Although they probably did. Seen from their point of view, it must look as if he had fallen into the most traditional, clichéd honey trap. A younger woman. Another life. Probably hated him already. Especially the youngest, the girl who no longer had a real father.

'I suppose we have to start being a bit more careful. Eat out less. I can do the cooking sometimes, you know,' he mentioned to Casey as they left the bank, where the money from England still hadn't arrived. More documents to be signed. Formalities. Legal mumbo-jumbo.

Casey sneered.

'Soon, you'll have me ironing your shirts,' she said.

Jake didn't answer,

'Let's have a coffee at Borders,' he suggested.

'Yes, I can look at some of the magazines. It'll save having to buy them,' Casey said.

'Please, don't be sarcastic. You know we can still afford magazines. It's not that bad. And when the cash from the sale comes through, we'll have nearly a hundred grand. We can splash out a bit, buy some new clothes. Maybe investigate a house on the Canals.'

'We'll never have enough,' Casey realistically pointed out.

And then there was the novel Jake promised he would write. Few of his previous books had ever earned out their initial advances, but this time he pointed out, it would be commercial, a moneymaker. 'And you can be my inhouse editor,' he promised Casey. Which only served to deepen her blue funk.

'I miss my job in London, Jake. Really. We never meet any one, here. We can't go on forever just the two of us. We'll bore each other, get bored together. And then what?'

They walked through the Santa Monica backstreets, away from the fashionable pedestrian centre of boutiques, cafés and giant malls. Past new age bookstores, comic shops, an out of the way branch of Tower Records, no longer holding hands like in the first days, trying to dissipate the mood of despondency. He bought her a red rose from a stall. She accused him of embarrassing her. She walked along faster, head down, shoulders tight, her long legs eating up the pavement. Jake kept up with her.

Sandwiched between a skateboard boutique and a Chicano grocery was a porno movie house down on its luck, car park almost empty, just a few dusty motorcycles and a lone saloon which badly needed a new paint job. It advertised two films for five dollars only.

'We can afford that, can't we, Jake?' Casey remarked. 'You always promised you would take me. Come on, now's the time.'

An old woman with a desultory chignon took his greenbacks, pressed a buzzer and the door to the theatre opened. They walked in. The lights were still on and there were just a half dozen spectators in there, all squirming in their seats as they saw Casey and her wild mane of blonde hair enter.

'Disappointing,' she said to Jake as they sat at the back. 'None of them have macs.'

'Wrong climate,' he remarked.

The auditorium, bathed in a strange cocktail of sweet smells and acrid disinfectant, went dark. A few of the other men shuffled uncomfortably in their seats in the rows ahead, adjusting their posture. Jake also felt ill at ease. Casey peered at the flickering screen as the clumsy typewritten credits rolled by.

'Wow,' she whispered. '*Black Anal Gang Bang*. Just what I wanted to see. Perfect.'

Her left hand moved over to Jake and she gripped his hand as the first images appeared.

It was more than sordid. Actually disgusting. There was no story at all, just this actually rather pretty young woman with long dark hair falling down over her shoulders, great purple lips and partly Asian eyes, body all white and compact, firm but unspectacular breasts and thin legs, in a room which reminded Jake of a photographer's studio he had once visited, black drapes everywhere in the background. As the film began, she was already nude, alone in the large room, when a knock on the door initiated the summary soundtrack. Her pubic area was carefully trimmed, to reveal a moist hairless gash, which she distractedly fingered as the camera zoomed in for a close-up of the darker outer lips. Jake knew he was getting hard already. Casey sensed this and lowered her hand onto his crotch.

This black guy entered, also nude. His penis was amazingly long and yet didn't even appear to be erect at this stage. The man and the woman embraced, mechanically. Soon, she took him in her mouth as he hardened. Surely she was going to choke on his member as it kept on expanding. Another black man came in through the door as she sucked away. This one was erect but smaller. He placed himself behind the dark-haired girl and kneeled as she worked away, his cock now pointing towards her backside. He spat in his hands and wetted his tip and quickly speared the young woman's backside. The camera moved to her face. She couldn't hide the pain. The man sodomising her now lifted her by the waist so she was on all fours and furiously began thrusting into her. It didn't last long and quickly he extricated himself from her bowels and spurted all over her back. The first man withdrew from her mouth, his member now majestic, monstrous and dripping with the girl's saliva. He positioned her, standing against an armchair and slowly corkscrewed into her rear. For a moment, Jake, fascinated, thought he would never fit as his appendage barely squeezed itself an inch or two into the woman s dilated aperture. But he kept on pushing forward until he was all in, buried inside her, stretching the girl's anus to all heavens and beyond as the second black man gently squeezed her nipples. The whole screen was now occupied by the pole of the dark penis moving in and out of her rear hole. Utter close-up where they could distinguish every protuberant, throbbing vein on his member and unsightly red pimples around her aperture, glistening fluids catching the light as the fucking continued. Casey unzipped Jake's jeans and pulled his now hard cock out and began jerking him off as she kept on watching the screen.

The pattern remained the same. The first black guy came outside her as a third acolyte entered the room and replaced him. By the end of the film, there were six men and all had tried her arsehole and discharged over her back. The girl was sweating profusely. At one stage, two of the smaller-membered men attempted to insert their cocks into her simultaneously, but neither of the trio could stay in that position very long and one of them kept sliding out. All the time, the soundtrack was a collection of sighs, deep breaths and would-be orgasmic moans, none very convincing.

Jake came as the fourth black man entered the woman's rear, but Casey kept on pulling on his penis, as if on automatic pilot, until he was completely empty. The film ended somewhat abruptly. The lights did not come back on and two men made a bee-line for the toilets. Jake's throat felt unbearably dry. Casey shoved his cock back into his trousers and zipped him up. The second film began. A blonde woman in a sports car was cruising some Californian highway. Casey stood.

'I've seen enough,' she said. 'Let's go.'

In the harsh daylight, Jake felt awfully self-conscious, the front of his trousers still damp from his ejaculation. They walked silently towards the car park. He just didn't know what to say, or think. Casey just looked forward as they moved on, her gaze fixed on the palm trees of the sea promenade a mile or so ahead.

Back at the apartment, the silence between them continued.

'That was interesting,' Casey finally said, breaking the ice. 'I never thought it would be possible to accommodate so much. Rather sordid, hey, Jake?'

'Quite,' he agreed.

'But it was also rather exciting, don't you think so?'

'I suppose so.'

'I know,' Casey said. 'Let's have some fun tonight. I want to do some real drinking. Let's go to some hotel near LAX. Those are the bars where all the action is supposed to be.'

They knew that from movies they'd seen.

It turned out to be a bar like any other. Shiny, anonymous, bottles, barman, faces.

The couple had been sitting in a corner. Nursing his soft drink as Casey started on her third vodka and orange, Jake had not even noticed them at first. Then he became aware of the woman watching him sip from his glass, with an enigmatic smile on her lips. Scarlet mouth, probably the same lipstick as Casey. The man came over to talk. Nothing very direct. Casey gently drunk, letting off some of the pressure of the last few weeks, talking about London and things and such. The guy worked for some studio and feigned interest when he heard of Jake's writing and Casey's publishing background. The woman was actually quite pretty, in an artificial sort of way, a bit plastic, big-breasted and all smiles. Good at small talk, Jake quickly noticed, who'd never had the patience for meaningless conversation even when in the best of moods.

He didn't remember whether it was the man or the woman who first suggested they move on to their suite for more drinks.

When the woman, Lucy, sitting next to him on the sofa nibbled his ear, Jake looked toward Casey, appealing for help, but she sat on the other couch with the studio executive's hand on her knee, impassive, acquiescent. The man pulled her skirt back and slipped a hand between Casey's thighs as Lucy unbuckled Jake's belt. They almost seemed to working in perfect synchronicity. Experience, no doubt. As Lucy's lips lowered themselves down on Jake's cock, he watched Casey and the other guy rise, their attire in disarray, and walk to the bedroom. Jake closed his eyes and to stay hard, imagined Casey in the other room as the other man fucked her, focusing like a camera on the sordid details, the flush rising over her cheeks, the anonymous penis brushing aside her curls and inserting itself between her pink lips, the changing colours of her nipples as the other man manipulated her. It all helped him to stay hard as Lucy avidly swallowed him, even though the knowledge of what was happening was sheer torture. As was the fact that Casey was allowing it all to happen.

In the morning, Casey emerged, unkempt, from the bedroom and shrugged him out of his couch dreams. He opened his eyes. There was a hardness about Casey's face, today, that scared him. He pushed Lucy aside, brushing his arm against her silicone breasts and their unnatural firmness and rose.

'Let's go, Jake.'

'Okay,' he said, picking his crumpled shirt up from the carpet.

'I feel cheap,' Casey said.

'Me too,' Jake agreed as they left the hotel.

'Casey, you re always doing it, leaving your toe nails in the bath tub. Please.'

'Fuck you, Jake. Where else do you want me to trim them, for God's sake.'

'In the bath is fine. But you could flush them away, surely?'

'Oh, Mr Perfect. What about that tummy of yours? You keep on saying you're going to tackle it, diet, slim, something. Sometimes, when you bend over, it's really obscene. Love-handles, more like love pumps!'

'Come on, don't exaggerate.'

'I'm not, I assure you, have a good look at yourself in the mirror, you'll see.'

'Anything else that displeases you, while we're on the subject?'

'Yes. There is.'

'Ah.'

'This habit you have of not shaving at the week-end. First of all, it looks ridiculous, all those flecks of grey. And it scratches me all the time when we fuck. I don't like it. If you want to screw, then shave beforehand.'

'Sure. I just didn't realise it annoyed you so much.'

'Well, now you know.'

'Peace, Casey. Please. I just don't know why you re so crabby sometimes. All these rows are so unnecessary, love. '

'And don't fucking call me "love" all the time. Just because you re so much older, it feels patronising like hell; like I'm your little girl, your pet. I'm not Jake. I'm not. '

'That's not what it's supposed to mean. Just being affectionate.'

'But don't treat me like a child. It's what always bothered me about us before, you see. The age difference. What the hell am I going to do, what will happen to me when you're gone, when you no longer want or are capable or screwing me, Jake? Tell me.'

'Look, I'm only fifty one. I've enough years left in me, I assure you. You're over thirty anyway. There's nothing wrong about it. It's a common age difference. Anyway, if anything were to happen, there's the joint account. And the funds from the sale of the company are definitely coming in a week or so. You'll be safe.'

'I know Jake, I know. Sorry I'm being such a bitch. It's just that sometimes I feel so cooped up here. Maybe we should try Austin or Seattle? You keep on talking about other cities. Why not? Maybe there's something about California that doesn't agree with me. There are days when you're in the study typing away, when I actually feel my brain shrinking, know what I mean. Gotta find something to do.'

'Learn to drive. You'll be more independent.'

'Maybe you're right.'

'So tell me, why did you get back home so late last night?'

Sheri, his new agent, had arranged for him to make a pitch at one of the minor studios. It was an idea he'd had for years now, about a group of English-speaking expatriates in Paris following the end of WW2. The years of the St Germain des Prés cellars, jazz clubs and existentialism. Lotsa sex, confused affairs, emotions galore and private drama. Juicy roles for both Hollywood new-comers and strongly-fancied French talent like Julie Delpy or Sophie Marceau who were looking for US careers. Jake had lived in Paris then, of course, but he was too young and had missed out on that particular scene, but he knew he had the right feeling and could recreate it without too much research and make the period live again.

It had gone well and they had promised a prompt answer. At worst, a Guild minimum for a couple of initial drafts. Enough spending money for at least a year, he reckoned, unwilling that he was to dip into the English capital in their account.

On the way back, he had made a detour in Malibu to buy that expensive skirt Casey had liked the other week from the poncy boutique near the highway. Yes, she would like it. He could already imagine himself draping the thin, colourful material around her long, tanned legs. The better to undress her later, he smiled as the car hummed along the coastal road.

He knew something was wrong the moment he parked on the back road, a couple of blocks either way from both the canals and their apartment. The windows were wide open and surf music blasted out loudly. Certainly not a CD from their growing collection. He rushed up the stairs to their level and unlocked the door. The noise inside was so loud he could have been a burglar and come and gone without being heard.

He made his way through the flat. Casey was not in the main room where the hi-fi boomed away, or the bedroom. He lowered the sound, heard moans and walked into the kitchen.

There on the table was Casey, undressed from the waist down, being fucked by a tall, bronzed Venice Beach creature with shocking pink spandex shorts bunched around his ankles as he furiously thrust in and out of her.

'Jesus, Jesus,' she kept on moaning, as the man's thick cock ravaged her in metronomic fashion, digging deep inside her, the kitchen table on which she was crucified shuddering dangerously under their combined weight.

Jake stood, dead silent, in the doorway, watching them. He was hypnotised by the jerky movement of the man's stump into Casey's cunt, noticing the moistness of their combined genitals, the colour of her outspread inner lips and the pulsing brown of the man's balls as they repeatedly bounced against Casey's elevated backside. And his finger dug deep inside her anus. Like a giant porno screen, not a sordid detail left unseen.

No.

Still, Jake watched.

He'd seen this guy before, pulling weights on Venice Beach. Christ, he even had his chest waxed. And his legs. What did she see in him?

Jake took a step back.

Still, the copulating couple hadn't noticed his presence.

Without disengaging from Casey, the beach bum held her by the waist and turned her round, her breasts squashed against the table's wooden surface as he increased his thrusts inside, doggie-style, her legs nonchalantly hanging downwards to the kitchen floor. Casey kept on moaning. Jake couldn't remember her being so active in their own past lovemaking, as her hands swept back and cupped the man's balls to accelerate his piston-like movements into her. He inserted a second finger into her rear, stretching her obscenely and smiled quietly as he took in the spectacle of his cock moving and out of her and the fingers penetrating her.

Jake felt sick, but there was nothing inside him to throw up.

Casey's red face turned and caught a glimpse of Jake, standing there in the doorway.

'Christ!' she exclaimed. More annoyance than guilt.

The man slowed down and his head moved round, acknowledging Jake. He didn't move out of Casey; simply stared at Jake.

Her brown eyes proffered no apologies nor defiance. Just acceptance.

She wet her lips, moving her tongue across the lipstick-less surface.

'I'm sorry, Jake. But I would rather you went into the other room. I don't want you watching.'

He meekly obeyed.

In the living room, he sat, empty of all feelings, still listening to the continuous moans drifting back from the kitchen as Casey mercilessly continued to take her pleasure, over the derivative strains of the surf music. Finally, the noises ceased, and for ten minutes or so, he heard them talking heatedly, but couldn't make out a single word of what they were saying.

Eventually, the two emerged from the kitchen. They were still naked, sweaty. Jake looked up at Casey's crotch. Her cunt lips were still dark red and engorged, and there were pearls of come dripping out and onto her inner thigh. He choked and had to rush past them to the sink where he finally managed to be sick.

When he returned, Casey had slipped a robe on and the beach bum now had his shorts back on, his genitals strongly outlined against the thin material.

'This is Timothy, Jake,' she finally said after a short period of awkward silence.

'I see,' was all he could say.

So this is the way it was going to end.

'He's a personal fitness instructor, I met him on the beach.'

'I see,' Jake repeated.

'He fucks me better than you used to, Jake. I'm sorry. It was never going to work, you know. The first weeks here, the time in London where we had to hide to do it, they were good, but this is different, you see. You always scared me a bit. I never knew what you were going to do. I suppose that's why I came to America with you, in the first place. But it was never what I really wanted out of life.'

Jake feebly smiled as he looked Timothy up and down, from bronzed rippling-muscled chest to chunky pole-like legs. His face was rather plain under the severe crewcut.

'I suppose there's a logic here,' Jake said.

'What logic?' Casey asked.

'He does look a bit like your husband. Only a bit dumber.'

Casey went red in the face and protested.

'Jake, that's not fair, just not fair.'

'I should have listened to you; how you always said you had a cold heart. I might have realised that if you could dump your husband, it would be all too easy to dump me, too.'

'Remember that first time?'

'What, the hotel by the airport, after I was already thinking you were never going to pick me up at Camden Town?'

'No, at the Conference.'

'Where I sat in the audience listening to you read that vile story and I got all wet when you came to that part about the ice cubes, and determined to find out more about you. Already day-dreaming and lustful of how it might be with you?'

'No. Before. I was in the lobby greeting arriving delegates. It was early in the morning. The hotel staff were also drifting in, some already in uniform, some not. That shabby car pulled up, and that nobody of a driver helped you pull your luggage from the backseat.'

'That was my husband.'

'I thought it was a minicab. And you breezed in through the hotel door. You never did kiss him goodbye. If you had, I might never have persevered…'

'I don't like kissing in public.'

'You were so bloody tall and gawky I thought you were a late-arriving hotel housemaid and remembered thinking how different you were and how I'd love to have my room cleaned by you.'

'Bloody cheek!'

'Then, only later, I found out who you actually were.'

'So?'

'A sheer vision, with that flowing blue dress with small white polka dots, fucking hell you were. I'll never forget that first time I caught sight of you. Moments like that can change lives, you know.'

'You're too sentimental, I swear.'

Impassive, Casey explained to Jake how he owed her a new beginning. It all made sense, he reckoned, in a particularly twisted way. But then he was a master of irony.

'I'll stay here, of course. But Timothy has agreed to take you. Haven't you?'

'Yes,' the other guy said.

'I'll give him a share of the money, I have to. You understand, Jake. It's the only way. If you were still around, I'd always worry about what you would do, you're a loose cannon and I can't run the risk of you running wild out there. Sometimes, you're reasonable, but when you're not, you're absolutely impossible. Can't trust you. No way. You'd be silent for months then be on the phone again, protesting, making threats, scheming, turning our sad story into some movie script or novel. I can't have that, you see. I need a fresh start.'

'I understand,' Jake answered.

'You're the past, and the past has to be left behind.'

'Please, Casey, spare me the clichés.'

He followed Timothy to his beach buggy which was parked nearby. Casey waved them both goodbye from the window of the bedroom. As she did so, her flimsy robe gaped open, a final vision of her small breasts, the dark beauty spot neighbouring her left nipple. Timothy drove off. Lincoln, toward the Santa Monica highway, North through Beverly Hills, a road overlooking the Valley. Night falling. A heavy heart. A gentle breeze drifting in from the sea, full of alien smells and distant memories.

'Where is it, Timothy?' Jake asked him as they drove deeper into the darkening night.

'In the glove compartment,' the beach bum replied.

'Have you ever used it before?' Jake enquired.

'Once, in self-defence, some coloured dudes in Orange County tried to mug me outside a bowling alley. Sure scared them away fast.'

'I'm sure you won't understand, Timothy,' Jake said. 'But this is all a bit too much like a bad movie, you know, the Hollywood Hills where the hookers and the serial killers roam at night...'

'No, I don't understand. So shut the fuck up.'

They left the vehicle away from the main road leading up the hill, and walked the rest of the way, Jake ahead of the other man, stumbling in the darkness, the gun pointing at his back all the way up the narrow path.

'Stop there,' Timothy ordered.

'Here?'

'Yes.'

'She'll leave you too, you know,' Jake said. 'She's just using you. When my money runs out, she'll move on.'

'I know,' Timothy said. 'But for now the cash and her will do.'

'At least you're a realist,' Jake remarked.

'Yeah.'

'So it's now?' Jake enquired.

'Seems to be.'

'Let me do it myself,' Jake asked. 'It'll look less suspicious. Casey and you might actually get away with it, this way. You, I don't care about, but I don't want Casey to end up in jail. For old time's sake, for all the good times, you understand?'

'Can I trust you?' Timothy asked.

'You can. There's nowhere else for me to go. I can't fight the tide any longer. I'm tired. Very tired.'

'No funny business,' said Timothy, handing Jake the gun, and swiftly placing himself behind him, away from the weapon's direction.

'Thanks,' said Jake.

And placed the nozzle inside his mouth, angled the gun upward, toward his brain.

'It won't hurt, it won't hurt,' he mumbled.

'Now, please, Jake,' said Timothy behind him.

Jake nodded and his finger closed on the trigger.

A Map Of The Pain

It all begins in Blackheath, in South East London. They are in the kitchen, chatting aimlessly while preparing the evening meal. He drones on about the cutbacks at the BBC and his fears for his job. She isn't really listening to him. Her mind is miles away, in a bed with another man who touches her in all the right places, in all the right ways, another man who has betrayed her so badly.

He moves over to the fridge. Opens it, searches inside.

The heat is oppressive. London has not seen the likes of it for years. And he still wears his tie.

'I don't think we have enough tomatoes for the salad,' he says.

Her husband the vegetarian.

She fails to answer.

'I said we're low on tomatoes.'

The information registers through a haze of mental confusion.

'I'll pop over to the 7-Eleven on the High Street,' she volunteers. 'They're still open. I should have bought more stuff over lunch at the Goodge Street Tesco. It won't take me long,' she says.

'I'll come along' her husband says. 'Keep you company.'

'No, it's alright,' she answers. 'You can prepare the dressing.'

He's always been good that way, willing to cook and do things in the kitchen. She picks up her shoulder bag, with her purse and the manuscript she's working on and walks out onto the mews.

The night air is stale and sticky. She is wearing her white jeans and an old promotional tee-shirt.

She walks at her usual jaunty pace past the Common. Toward the shops. And breezes past the convenience store where a few spotty youths are squabbling by the ice-cream counter, and a couple of drab, middle-aged men are leafing through the top shelf girlie magazines. She heads on to the railway station. Network South East. The next train to Charing Cross is in five minutes. She uses her monthly Travelcard.

At the London station, she calmly collects her thoughts. Smiles impishly at the imagined face of her husband, waiting all this time for the final ingredients for the salad, back at their house. She catches the tube to Victoria and connects with the last train departure to Brighton.

Once, with her lover, she had gone there for a weekend, yeah a dirty week-end, she supposes. It was on the eve of a political party conference and the seaside resort had been full of grim-faced politicians and swarms of television journalists. She'd spent most of her time outside the hotel room where they had fucked more times than she had thought possible in the space of 36 hours, absolutely terrified of venturing across her spouse, or some colleagues of his who might be familiar with her, even though he worked on the business and economics side and she well knew he could not be in Brighton right then.

Katherine spent the night ambling up and down the seafront, enjoying the coolness of the marine breeze and sea air after the Turkish bath of her London suburbs and the publisher's offices where she worked. It was wonderfully quiet; no drunks to accost her, just alone with her thoughts, the memories, the scars of lust, the mess that her life now was.

Her lover had betrayed her. And she, in turn, had betrayed both men.

She wanted to wipe her mind clean of everything, to erase the wrong-doing and the pain she had inflicted on them. To start anew, like a baby arriving into the world, free of fault, innocent, like a blank tape ready for a new set of experiences, a new life almost.

In the morning, she booked herself into a small bed and breakfast on a square facing the old pier. She shopped for new clothes, which she paid for by credit card. She ate fish and chips, like a tourist and even found the Haagens-Dazs ice-cream parlour she remembered from a previous visit to one of the backstreets. Maraschino cherry delight. The weather was warm but nowhere near as bad as London. On the promenade, she bought a floppy straw hat to protect her pale skin from the fierce sun. She took a nap in the afternoon in the cramped room of the small hotel. Before dozing off, she had switched the TV on and seen her husband on screen looking all jolly and smug on the business lunch programme, reporting from the car park of an automotive parts factory. It had been recorded two days earlier. She awoke later from a dream-free sleep, enjoyed a leisurely bath during which she depilated her legs and cut her toe nails, and, clean and refreshed, slipped on the new lightweight dress she had purchased earlier, low-cut, dark blue with white polka dots, billowing away down over her long legs from a high waist.

'First night away,' she remarked to herself, as she walked out into the dusk.

She meets this guy in a pseudo-Texan Cantina. He says he's from one of the unions. She's had a couple of beers, and he offers her a glass of tequila. It burns her throat and stomach.

'I canvas for Labour locally, where I live,' she tells him, to indicate that at least they share the same political affiliation. She's always suspected, despite his indifferent denials, that that bastard of a lover she'd been involved with had actually voted Tory. How in hell could she have slept with him?

He smiles at her, well, more of a leer really.

So what? she thinks.

She follows him, his name is Adam Smith, back to the bar of the Old Ship where he is staying for the conference. It's already pretty late, and there are only a handful of people left in the penumbra of the bar. She has a couple of vodka and oranges. Her head feels light. Better this than the heavy burden of all the memories and the guilt, she reckons.

'Is that a wedding ring?' the guy enquires, pointing at her finger.

'Yes,' she answers. 'Does it bother you?'

It all floods back. How her lover would delicately slip both the wedding and the thin engagement rings off her fingers before ceremoniously undressing her from top to bottom, before they would make love in the basement to the sound of the whirring fan and the light of the long-life candle she herself had bought near the Reject Shop on Tottenham Court Road.

'No, I was just wondering, that's all,' he remarks.

'If it bothers you, I can take them off,' Katherine says.

'No, no,' he says, annoyed by this turn of events. But while he is still saying this, she has already wet her finger and slipped both the rings off, deliberately dropping them at the bottom of her glass.

'Satisfied?' she asks.

Is she drunk, he wonders? 'They'll be closing the bar any minute, I reckon,' he says, ignoring her earlier remark. 'Can I entice you up to my room for a final nightcap?'

She isn't drunk. Just a bit lost, she guesses. She looks at this man called Smith of all things. His tie isn't straight, his shirt has a few drink stains, scattered across its front. She can read him like a map. But what the hell?

'Yeah, why not?' she answers, grabbing her bag still loaded with the manuscript from her old life, and stands up, abandoning the rings in the half-empty glass of booze.

As he inserts the electronic card into the door, he leers at her again. Why must he be so obvious, Katherine thinks?

The door swings open.

He stands aside and Katherine walks in.

The room is medium-sized, dominated by a large king-size bed. A door on the right leads to a bathroom. On the walls, anonymous prints of naval victories from the Napoleonic wars. She smiles; it might have been worse: it could have been the classic print of the Eurasian woman with the blue face. If it had been, she thinks she might have walked straight out again.

He follows her in and the door slams quietly.

He walks to the bedside table where a large bottle of scotch stands, no, bourbon. Four Roses.

He takes his jacket off. His shirt is straining at the waist, his girth stretching the button holes.

'Drink?' Adam suggests.

She hates the stuff but answers 'Why not?' That's how it's supposed to go, isn't it?

'So,' he sits down on the edge of the orange-brown bedspread, loosens his tie. 'How much?'

'How much what?' She hesitantly sips the harsh booze from the glass.

'How much do you charge? All that married woman crap doesn't cut much ice, you know. I don't care, I'll pay the going rate.' He takes a thick black leather wallet from the inside pocket of his jacket. Opens it and pulls out two fifty pound notes.

Katherine notices there are quite a lot more where they came from.

He hands her the cash. 'Okay,' she says, taking it.

She stands to begin undressing.

He smiles.

She unzips the dress where it cinches her waist and pulls it up above her head. And off. All she is wearing is her underwear. The black bustier and knickers set and the matching suspender belt and dark stockings. What she always wore for the assignments with her lover. Her skin is pale, her tummy flat like a marble table, her thighs full, the tight suspender belt biting in to the skin above her hips.

She moves to unhook the bustier but Adam interjects: 'No, keep your top on. You haven't got much up there. I'd rather you didn't.'

She stands there, legs apart, wondering what to do next. Thinking, why am I so passive? I know what I'm doing. Fleetingly, she remembers how, one night, in the thrall of rapture, he had whispered in her ear: 'One day, Kate, you will walk all the sexual stations of the Cross, you see'. At the time, she hadn't quite understood, but had found it sexy, him saying things like that, it fired her lust up even more. Now, she was beginning to understand.

He gulps down the contents of his glass. She obliges, doing the same. He pours more bourbon.

'Well?' she asks.

'Take your pants off,' the union representative demands.

Katherine unhooks a stocking, but the guy interrupts:

'No, keep your stockings on.'

She bends and pulls the knickers down, slipping the thin fabric across the nylon and over her flat shoes. She leaves the garment on the hotel room floor and straightens up again.

Her pubic curls lie flattened against her damp skin. He gazes at her lower stomach, all traces of his smile now disappearing as he drinks in the sight of her nudity.

'Come here,' he says. She moves closer to him, her cunt facing his eyes, as he remains in the chair.

His fingers invade her thatch, spreading the dark curls. He slips a finger into her gash. Probes.

'You're not very wet, are you?'

Katherine stays silent.

He withdraws his finger from her sex. Brings it up to his nose, sniffs. Grunts.

'Suck my cock.'

He unzips his fly.

Katherine kneels by the chair. He pulls his penis out. It's semi-erect, pinker than others she has come across. Not that she's encountered that many. A handful of clumsy groping sessions and fucking in the darkness at University, following alcoholic parties, and then her husband, uncircumcised and reliably sturdy, and five years later the damn lover, circumcised, thicker, darker, pulsating, veined like a tender tree. Life as an interrupted parade of male members!

She takes the man's cock between her fingers, pulls on the foreskin and the glans emerges, reddish, the colour of fever. She lowers her head, opens her lips and takes the member into her moist insides. He's not too big. She hates it when it makes her choke. Her tongue slowly makes contact with the swelling penis, circles its extremity; he tastes different, a slightly acrid, sweaty odour, musk and urine. Suddenly, she feels his hand on her head, fingers burrowing into her thick curls, pressuring her mouth to go deeper and swallow his cock up to its hairy hilt. The tip of her tongue dallies over the cock's small hole. When she touches him there, there's a trembling, a nervous shudder that courses through his whole body. She senses he is about to come and sucks harder on his now fully-grown member. He tries to hold back but she stimulates the base of his cock with her fingers while her tongue relentlessly keeps on teasing his opening.

'You bitch,' he sighs, aware that she is trying to finish him off. Expediting the job.

But the surge can't be halted, and within a few seconds his whole body spasms. As this happens, Katherine opens her mouth wide to disengage herself from his throbbing cock, but he viciously holds her head down even harder and comes inside her mouth. She gags on the hot stream of come and has no other choice than to swallow the stuff. Bastard, she mutters under her breath. It sticks in her throat. She feels like being sick. Finally, he releases his hold on her head and she is allowed to pull her mouth back. She wipes her lips with the back of her hand, to eliminate the lingering taste of his seed.

His quickly shrivelling penis still dangling like a marionette from his open trousers, he gets out of the chair before she has time to stand up again and signals her to the bed. She sits on the edge, and he forces her down so that her long legs dangle over the side. He lowers himself down to the carpet, and sticks two fingers into her cunt.

'Still dry, hey?' he says, forcing his way past her labia.

She looks down at him, his face at cunt-level, thinning hair bobbing up and down between her thighs. She distractedly notices there's a ladder near the knee of her left stocking. How did that happen, she wonders?

His fingers slip in and out of her sex. She has no feeling of excitement. This is what being an object is, she reckons.

'Your cunt hair is too long,' he tells her, parting the curls around her opening.

'I don't go to the barbers very often,' she attempts a feeble joke.

'Wait there. Don't move,' he says, rising and moving over to the settee where a battered attaché-case lies. He opens it and pulls out a nail kit and a small pair of scissors.

He pulls on her pubic curls, untangling the longer ones and trims the extremities along a straight line. It feels funny. She looks down after he has completed the work. Her bush is now distinctly thinner, and the lips of her sex are plainly visible behind the growth.

'There, that's nicer, isn't it?' he remarks. 'Now you can see the merchandise.'

She doesn't answer.

'I want to see inside,' he says. 'Use your own fingers. Open up.'

She obeys.

He peers inside her, his eyes piercing her innards.

Her lover used to say that her insides were the colour of coral. She closes her eyes.

'I'm going to fuck you now,' Adam says. 'Where do you keep your condoms? In your handbag?'

'I don't have any,' Katherine replies. 'I've already told you, I'm not a whore.'

'Bloody hell,' the man says. 'Shit. You don't think I'm gonna put my cock inside there; I don't know where you've been before.'

'You didn't mind my mouth,' she says, a tad angrily. 'That was good enough for you, wasn't it?'

Only five cocks before, she thinks. A bloody woman of experience... No, not even, the first two she never gave head to.

She looks at this man, and finds him ridiculous. Overweight, standing there with his small cock peering out between the curtains of his half-open trousers.

She giggles.

He reacts badly and slaps her across the cheek.

'Don't...'

'I've paid. I'll do exactly what I want to do, woman.'

'Bastard.'

He slides his belt out of the trouser top, and she's totally unprepared for this, as he grabs both her wrists and binds them together. Tight. She's too slow to react. Vulnerable, obscenely undressed in front of this stranger with her cunt wide open, her black stockings in disarray, her small breasts feeling heavy inside the cups of the bustier, her cheek still on fire from the blow. Adam pulls her by her bound wrists towards the bathroom, pushes the door open with his foot.

Katherine is frightened. What now? She has read too many serial killer novels. For Christ's sake, she edits them. In her bag over at the bed and breakfast, there's even a manuscript for one that takes place in Arizona. *Fiction editor found slaughtered in Brighton hotel.* Will he slit my throat and arrange my mutilated body in a pornographic vision that goes beyond obscenity? Will he carve off the tips of my breasts, insert the carving knife in my cunt and slit me all the way up like a chicken? Will he cut my labia off and display them partly-chewed inside my open mouth?

She shudders.

He pushes her down on the toilet.

'There,' he says.

'Yes?' she enquires.

'I want you to pee, and I want to watch. Come on, open those legs wide, wider, now. Come on. Show me that piss squirting out of you.'

'No,' she says.

'Yes.'

'Undo my hands, then maybe. If I can manage it.'

He does. She tries.

Katherine has never peed in front of a man, of any one. She blushes intensely. Closes her eyes and concentrates. He fills a toothbrush mug with water and forces her to swallow. And again. She can feel the warmth inside her stomach, the muscles tensing. He keeps on standing there, silent now, watching entranced the quivering, moist entrance to her cunt.

Finally, the flow is unleashed. The odorous liquid flows.

It feels both painful, like a particularly strong period bursting from her and rupturing some remote part of her body, but also pleasurable, like a fourth division orgasm, a satisfying but unremarkable feeding of the lust inside, not unlike the routine lovemaking she had been having for ages with her husband.

Adam watches as the thin stream of pee first dribbles out, then streams arc-like into the bowl, emerging from the thin opening between her cunt lips. As she tightens her throat, he approaches a finger, allows the liquid to pearl over it like a cascade, and inserts it suddenly into her pouring aperture. Then another finger, yet another and savagely stretching the muscles inserts his whole fist into her. Katherine screams in agony. But the windows of the hotel room are closed and Brighton doesn't hear.

Finally, the flow stops and he withdraws his hand. It still hurts and she is about to cry, as he slaps her face again and cries out:

'You bitch, you enjoyed that, didn't you.'

She nods.

'Stick a finger up your arse.'

She makes a gesture of protest but he swings the belt close to her cheek.

He pulls her off from the toilet bowl, pushes her onto her knees, on all fours. Manipulates her so that her rump points upward and guides her right hand (how could he know she was left-handed?) toward the dark cranny of her anus.

'Now,' he says.

To urge her on, he places his foot above her other hand, as if to tread on it.

She slowly inserts her middle finger into the puckered aperture. The ring of muscles rebels against the intrusion and she barely manages half a nail.

'More,' Adam says, and steps harder onto her free hand.

She pushes the finger harder. The ring of flesh relaxes. She feels another need to pee, but holds back. Finally, the finger plants itself deep inside her arsehole, spearing herself up to its first joint. The feeling is not unpleasant.

'Dirty girl, hey? Slut.'

She looks up at him.

'Take it out.'

She does.

'Lick it clean.'

She does.

Then, despite her tired protests, he binds her hands together again with the leather belt and pulls her back toward the bedroom. She stumbles and he allows her to fall over the settee. He stands back and says:

'Yeah, that's it. Keep your legs wide open. I'm still going to fuck your brains out, you know. I can get condoms on room service, if I want. Whenever I want. Bitch.'

He takes a swig from the bottle of bourbon and sits back on the bed, smugly watching her spread-eagled across the settee, her genitals in technicolour display like a centrefold in a skin magazine.

'Whenever I want,' drinking from the bottle again.

Half an hour later, he has fallen asleep and Katherine manages to untie the belt and liberate her hands. She dresses hurriedly, abandoning the black knickers she's had to wipe her moist crotch with. She feels soiled, violated like never before. The man s jacket is draped over the chair by the door. She pulls out his wallet and takes all the cash. At least six hundred pounds.

Softly, softly into the Brighton night.

It's now New York.

Autumn has come, or rather Fall as they call it over there.

Katherine has travelled to Manhattan and found a drab, cheap room in an equally cheapo rundown hotel a few blocks off Times Square, where she often has to jostle with local prostitutes in the somewhat seedy reception area, she picking up her keys – there are never any messages, they booking in their furtive johns. Soon, the working girls begin to recognise her and become friendly. The sultry weather is fading fast. She spends mornings in the Park, reading older books, Dickens, Thomas Hardy, all the novels she should have studied better when she was at Cambridge, where she'd got her 2.2 because of a silly indulgence where she had written mock haikus for one of her assigned essays. She'd deserved a 2.1 at least, she knew, her tutor had said so, but she'd also wasted too much time at pointless parties and playing ingenues badly in college plays. Sitting calmly in the sparse grass, the rumour of the traffic distant, the top edge of the surrounding skyscrapers just about visible from her vantage point, she thinks of the past. Over and over. How she first betrayed her trusting if rather dull husband with a dangerous lover, who soon became too possessive, too disturbing, until she felt she had to break things off and he went berserk. He'd always wanted to bring her to New York, she remembered. How frightening the day he had told her he had already purchased tickets for them, two or three months ahead in time, and served her with this ultimatum to come to America with him and not return to her husband. She'd panicked.

For her lover to exact a desperate vengeance in the way of men who have projected their deepest fantasies upon a muse only to feel betrayed by their ordinary, selfish and fallible humanity. Yes, he was one for muses. What did he see in her? Why her? She knew she wasn't worth it. She didn't have his sense of romance, she had a cold heart, she had prosaic aspirations but then what else could she have desired with a husband who wore a suit and tie as if it were a lifetime achievement and though a couple of years younger than her, looked and acted as if he were already in his forties?

She closed her copy of *A Tale Of Two Cities* and sighed.

Soon, she'd finish the book and would need something new to read. This afternoon, she could walk down Fifth Avenue to the Village, past the Flatiron Building and onto Broadway, to Tower Books on Lafayette. Soon, she also knew she would be running out of money. The Brighton cash was already dangerously low and the hotel's weekly bill would exhaust it in a few days. By now, she supposed, her credit card must be invalid. And even it if weren't, she did not wish either of the two absent men to find out where she might be.

She gathered her few belongings, putting the now empty diet Coke can into the brown paper bag together with the well-fingered paperback, strapped on the shoulder bag in which she kept her passport, diary and the remaining cash and headed for Central Park South. She wore a white and red tee-shirt advertising a London mystery bookstore and a wrap-around skirt of many colours, both of which she'd found in a Goodwill thrift store near 22nd Street, shortly after her arrival here.

A detour on the walk back to the hotel and she moved down 46th Street, past all the jewellery stores towards the Gotham

Book Mart, where the second-hand stock was often reasonably priced. None of the books, however, caught her fancy today and she crossed the Avenue of the Americas and continued toward the bustle of Times Square. Tourists queued impatiently at the reduced price theatre ticket kiosk. She ignored all the British accents among the Babel-like cacophony of the conversations.

The yellow taxis roared down Broadway as she crossed the main road under the shadow of the gigantic neon displays. Katherine looked up. There, that's where the black girl at the hotel had said it would be. A fading sign: *Girls Wanted For Burlesque Show*. On both sides of the small theatre's entrance were large emporiums selling all the latest video and electronic junk.

She ignored the Israeli salesmen aggressively pitching their wares to any tourist lingering long enough outside and walked through the side entrance into the building.

'My friend Lisa sent me,' Katherine says.

The little guy smoking an evil-smelling cigar lounges back in his chair and looks her over. At the front of his cluttered desk is a board with his name: *Guy N Bloom*. The office smells of damp and old newsprint. On the wall, old kitsch posters of past vaudeville shows coexist with full-colour spreads of more recent, and explicit beefcake, tanned women flashing obscenely gaping pink split beavers, many of them signed *To Guy, my favorite guy* and other such witticisms.

'Your top,' he indicates.

Katherine pulls the white tee-shirt over her head, her breasts fall free, she hasn't been wearing a bra. She's never really needed to wear one.

The response is predictable.

'Not much up there, hey?' the older man says.

'I know I'm not very voluptuous, but...' she begins to say.

'I like your accent, though. Limey, hmm?' He smiles. A mask of kindness almost invades his lined features. 'Tell you what, you look a bit Irish to me. Pull your hair back, all those curls, there's too many of them.'

She follows his instructions and bunches her myriad curls together and pulls the thick clump back to reveal her forehead. She doesn't like herself like this, her forehead is too large.

'Interesting,' says Bloom. 'You're not really that beautiful, but you've got something, you know. You're different; I think the guys might well like you. Pity about the tits, though. Turn round and give me a looksie.'

She does.

'No need to take it all off, just pull the skirt up. Let me see your butt. Yeah, thought so, great legs, honey, ass is a bit big, very white, not seen much tanning. Definitely, they'll like you.'

He explains the terms of employment.

'How much money you make is up to you. The better you are, the more they like you, the more tips you'll get. It's all tips. We don't pay any insurance, so you look after yourself. You supply your costume, or lack of costume should I say...' he sniggers.

'No funny business inside the theatre. What you arrange outside is your own business, and I don't want to know anything about it. Understood?'

'Yes, I understand,' Katherine says. 'When can I start? I really need some money. Bills to pay, you know.'

'First shift starts tomorrow at two, honey. I might actually come and have a look myself, you're different, should be interesting. Sometimes I regret I'm no longer a young man. Maybe your bump and grind routine will be more intelligent than the other gals. Show some imagination.'

Of course, Katherine thinks, I have a degree in English from Cambridge, what do you expect?

And thinks one brief moment of her erstwhile lover, who made such a song and melodramatic fuss after she had rejected him of the fact he had never seen her dance. Well now, honey, you'd have to pay, she says under her breath.

The other girls explain how to string the whole thing together. Katherine has bought herself a spectacular bikini, spandex or something like it, shiny, leather-like, and another dancer, a girl with a pronounced Tennessee drawl lends her a feather boa and some silk scarves and show her how best to drape them around her body. In the cramped dressing-room, she slaps on her best scarlet lipstick and loses one of her soft contact lenses, the last one from the old British prescription. The floor is filthy and she can't find it again. She takes the other out. Things are blurry now. At least, she won't see all the bloody men in the audience too close. A saving grace.

'Have you chosen your tunes?' another dancer asks Katherine.

'What tunes?'

'You know, kiddo, the music you want to dance to.'

Kiddo. The girl under all her flaky make-up is barely out of her teens. Worn before her years. Katherine will soon turn thirty. She reckons she might well be the oldest here. Never mind.

'I hadn't thought of it, really. I'll dance to anything they play.'

'Here, use this,' the girl says, handing her a CD. 'It's great, but the rhythm is not really me. You have it, you use it.'

Katherine peers at the label. *Shake* by the Vulgar Boatmen.

She waits in the wings, watches the first three girls do their numbers. She can't believe it. They are lewd, provocative, dirty, wonderfully indecent. She can't do any of this. Really, she can't. What am I doing here? In Times Square, cesspool of the western world, where a few doors away a derelict cinema is still screening *Deep Throat* and black pimps sashay down the street like living clichés, and there's Bruce Springsteen's *Candy's Room* booming in the air as the black girl gyrates on stage and bends and stretches her body to an impossible degree and the time comes and Katherine holds her breath back and makes her way to the illuminated stage.

'Go, blondie, go,' shout the other dancers as she reaches the centre of the proscenium. They sense it's her first time and show solidarity.

But the music doesn't start, and she stands there, paralysed, crucified under the dual assault of two glaring, hot spotlights, her medusa curls held aloft by the conditioning mousse, her shiny underwear glittering, her legs long and white, all the bruises from back in London now faded away. She wets her lips. Tries to see the audience and can only distinguish a few trouser legs emerging from the outlying darkness. Not even a dirty mac in sight.

A guitar chord and the song begins.

She swings her hips to the beat, pulls the green silk scarf draped over her shoulder across to her throat, caresses the material as it lingers there, a fragile noose of fabric, her knees bend to the rhythm, her bare feet drag slowly across the stage floor, she closes her eyes one moment, pulls with her free hand on the other scarf circling her wrist and waves it in the air where it floats slowly, suspended like a slow-motion kite during the festival at Blackheath; the scarf swims down and lands on the gentle rise of her breasts. She dances in one spot, her body circling the area in a steady motion, every breath in her soul singing parallel to the melodic waves of the rock and roll tune. Her fingers linger over the silk square now protecting her pale chest, she slides them down the narrow slope, from the brown mole at the onset of her cleavage to the tip of her left breast, where she rubs the still concealed aureola through the recalcitrant plastic-like thickness of the bikini bra. Katherine remembers the bump and grind tradition and, when the beat accelerates, with an artificial smile piercing her scarlet lips she pushes her bum out, and then her crotch. Dance, girl, dance. She takes hold of the silk scarf still draped over her chest, slips it between the thin strap and pulls it across the valley separating her two slight promontories, and out again, throws the piece of fabric in the air and allows it to drift down to the stage floor where she kicks it away just a few inches with her toe, as her hips keep gyrating mechanically to the music which seems to be growing louder and louder. She unclips the bra and loosens her breasts, soon to cover them chastely with the other silk piece until now adorning her throat like a thin choker. She feels her nipples growing erect under the thin gauze. Her body undulates steadily as she lowers both her hands and begins to gently massage her nipples through the fabric, like she saw the other women do before and when the chorus of the song jumps in, she pulls the silk piece away to reveal her front unencumbered. A few claps in the sparse crowd. She dances on, Salome of only two veils. She can feel sweat rising through the pores of her unveiled skin. A clammy feeling under her armpits where she had shaved only yesterday afternoon. Her upper lip, which she'd bleached at the same time, itches. The beat goes on. Come on, baby, give us more skin. She dances on, trying somehow to lose herself inside the relentless music. Bump and grind. Push your bum out; shove that crotch forward, show them how the mound of your cunt stretches the fabric of the bikini bottom. Bump. Grind. Push. Shove. The song ends. Another begins without a pause for breath or reflection. Every stage number is divided into three ritual parts, three songs or pieces of music. The new tune is an old big band blast. Brassy. She quickens the movement of her wavering shoulders and the geometrical patterns her arms are tracing in the glare of the harsh spotlights. She moves two steps forward, closer to the edge of the stage where small coloured bulbs imprint rectangular patterns of gaudy colours over the white skin of her legs. As her hands keep on caressing her breasts, she feels a tremor in the pit of her stomach. She recognises it, the onset of lust. Like when they were in his office, clandestine adulterers and she knew he was about to pull his underwear down and release his thick, dark, tasty cock. She opens her eyes to chase away the dream of the past and for the first time sees, albeit in a myopic blur, the eyes of some of the men in the audience. Hungry. Malevolent. Get on with it, they say. Katherine slips her fingers under the elastic of the bikini bottom. Pulls the garment an inch away from the flesh of her stomach. Tease them a bit, she thinks. A cavalcade of pianos attack the chorus and she swiftly pulls the knickers down. She now stands fully nude, her hips and shoulders still adhering to the syncopated whirlpool of the big band sound. Isn't the song over yet? She doesn't feel sexy at all. She feels very much alone.

She has never stood nude before in front of more than a single man; never even skinny-dipped or gone to a nude beach. How many are there in the audience? She peers sideways into the stage wings. The other girls are no longer watching. But Bloom is, the damn cigar still hanging from his lips. She can't read the expression on his face from where she stands. She twirls around, remembers the wooden pole over there on the far side of the stage. Waltzes toward it. Shove. Bump. Thrust. Grind. Her body feels wet, the sweat must be pouring down her back, there's no air, the spotlights are so fucking hot, Jesus, the sweat must be sliding down between the crack of her arse. She reaches the pole and grabs it; her hands are moist as she circles the pole and sketches a few new improvised dance moves like a medieval virgin courting a maypole. The apparatus is in fact metallic. She grinds against it. The hard, round circumference mashes against her pubes, she places her breasts against it and it fills her valley. The song never ends. She throws her head back, the delicate orbs of her breasts stand free, firm, shiny under the film of sweat, she bends at the waist and blushes instantly as she senses her vagina gape open as she does this. But the audience can't see, she's too far from the front rows. She stands again. Dance. Dance until the end of time, Kate. She wriggles her backside, keeps on massaging her breasts, if only to keep her hands busy, the movement is quite mechanical as if she were spreading soap or foam over her chest. Yes, yes, he did do that when they had shared their first bath tub. The song ends. One more to go. A familiar riff splits the brief silence. The Rolling Stones. *Satisfaction*. Much too fast, what is she going to do now? For encores? She has to continue, do more. Needs the tips. Show them more. She moves back to the edge of the stage, dances with exaggerated languor as she mentally rakes up the good times, the bad times, the wedding in the chapel of their old college in Cambridge. Her left hand moves from breast to navel, and she pushes it deep with a corkscrew motion into the narrow pit of her belly button. A guy in the audience whoops and hollers. The other hand also abandons the tender nipple it had been tending and hovers over her sex. She swivels her hips like a belly dancer. The finger parts the hair, the darker curls, tip-toes like a scalpel across the now moist aperture. The other hand joins it soon and holds the lips open. She's so wet, it must be dripping onto the stage floor. She squats on her haunches and deliberately inserts one finger deep inside her cunt, as the guys in the front row open their eyes wider than they ever thought they could. She can no longer hear the music. Keith Richards must still be playing. She moves the finger deep inside, impales herself on it while a finger from her other hand squeezes her protruding clitoris. A hand emerges from the audience, holding a green bill. Closer, girl, closer. She inches her cunt forward until she's in a precarious equilibrium on the very edge of the stage. The man, whose face remains in the shadows, slides the money into her gaping cunt. She inches her way back. Stands up, the bank note sticking out from her innards. Dances. Bumps. Grinds. Thrusts. The audience whistles, applauds loudly. The music has now ended. Lisa, the black girl who'd sent her here, is waiting over there by the side of the stage to do her turn. Katherine bows to the invisible men in the darkness. Her audience. She pulls the note out from her vagina, half of it is soaking wet with her juices. She waves it. The men shout all sorts of things at her. She sticks two fingers back inside, twists them round to further loud yelps and brings them to her mouth where she licks them clean. Prisoners of lust, he had once described their fatal liaison. The stage lights dim and she can make out more of the meagre audience. There's only a dozen of them, but the noise they're making is enough to fill a soccer stadium. She recalls Brighton and Adam Smith, turns round and gets down on all fours and, sobbing gently, thrusting her rump out toward the anonymous men, she cruelly pushes her still lubricated finger into her arsehole. She's about to pull it out and show them how she can also lick shit like the best of sinners when Bloom and two of the other burlesque dancers hurriedly pull her off stage to the loud protests of the screaming guys.

'Are you crazy?' Bloom screeches at her. 'You fucking slut, you want to get us closed down?'

The girls all look at her as if she were insane.

'Goddam limey. She's deranged, a freak, you be must be sick to get your rocks off this way.'.

'Get her outta here. I don't want to see this woman again. She's downright crazy. Out.'

They bundle her into her day clothes.

Back on Times Square, a thin rain falling, likely to mess up her perm, Katherine unclenches her fist and extracts the bank note. It's a hundred.

Certainly worth a few more miles on the clock, on the road to nowhere.

In Miami, she discovered some men had long, thin cocks and all-over tans.

On alternate days, Katherine cruised the clubs and discos in the art deco district of Miami Beach, window shopping like any other tourist, quenching the ambient heat with a steady diet of cold sodas and ice-creams, while on others she worked a few continuous shifts in a shady strip joint — here, they no longer called them burlesques — all the way up the less fashionable area in the Northern reaches of Collins Avenue, beyond the Avventura Mall, where the highway to the Everglades began. Now, she'd perfected her act. Kept it simple, cleanly sexy, beyond the temporary madness, the excesses of Times Square. She grew accustomed to shaking her gangly body, grinding her crotch with a grimace feigning ecstasy against the metal of the central pole, thrusting her white, square butt toward the punters, teasing the vociferous crowd, keeping her legs together, letting her hands do the roving, a mechanical spectacle tailored to the unsatisfactory pop songs she had thread together to punctuate her movements.

The nights were long and empty in her room at the beachside inn. The paint on the wall flaked in places creating ever-changing Rorschach tests in the humid penumbra. Six in the morning was always the worst time, and time and again she had to control herself and not pick up the pink telephone and dial London. But which one? Which past man? And then always remembered the time difference. And anyway what would she say? Sorry? I'm really sorry, but I don't want to come back. She read a lot. At Bookstar they deep discounted and the other day, even though she couldn't really afford a hardcover – she's not getting very good tips — she had indulged and bought the new Anne Tyler novel, which she read in small doses, to stretch the pleasure.

Sunday is her day off and like a good working girl she went to the beach, with a basket of fruit and a cold box full of drink cans. She's got this new rather daring outfit, with a thong cutting deep into her crotch, separating the two globes of her backside like a piece of meat. But she always kept her top on. Her husband would approve. Her skin burns easily, so she has to shield carefully under a parasol. The sand gets everywhere, as she ritually turns onto her stomach, then her back and again her stomach, and tried to concentrate on her reading. She knew that later she would have to use the shower nozzle against all her cavities to excavate the millions of small grains stuck to her perspiring skin, nestled between her bum cheeks and even inside her vagina.

This rugged-looking man walked by her parasol, briefly obscuring the sun. Out of the corner of her eyes, she saw his feet in the sand just a few inches away from her towel.

'*Guapa muchacha*,' he said with a strong Hispanic accent.

Katherine looked up.

'Hi,' she said.

'You're not from here,' he remarked.

'No, I'm not.'

He sat himself down next to her; he wore a silk shirt with exotic rainbow patterns and baggy trousers cinched at the waist.

'Let me have a guess,' he smiled.

Katherine smiled back.

'I know, you're Australian. I saw that movie, you know.'

She burst out laughing, her hand flying up, lost her page as the book fell into the sand and closed.

'You look a bit like Nicole Kidman, the chick who married Tom Cruise.'

'So I'm told. It's all the curls, you see. But no, I'm not from down under. I'm English, you see,' she explained.

'No kidding,' the man said. 'I'd never have guessed. You look more Swedish, or Dutch, you know.'

'Actually Irish a generation or two back,' she said.

'Very beautiful,' he flashed ivory white teeth that must have cost a small fortune in dental care.

'Thank you.'

He took her hand in his, shook it and introduced himself:

'My name is Steve Gregory,' he revealed.

'That's a very American name,' she pointed out.

'Well, not really, it's Gregorio. Esteban Gregorio. But I changed it. Came over from Cuba. What about you?' he asked her.

'Eddie,' she said.

English Eddie was her stage name. Her damn mother had insisted on making her second name Edwina.

'That's wonderful,' he exclaimed and offered her a cigarette.

A hundred meters away, the sea murmured and the waves of the Caribbean lapped the warm shore.

Katherine sighed.

Steve had brown eyes. Dangerous eyes. The sort she'd seen before, the type of eyes that could make her do things she shouldn't. The top buttons of his shirt were open to reveal an abundant growth on his brown chest. She surprised herself by looking down at his trousers and the strong bulge there, and thinking what sort of shape his cock must be.

Later, he took her for a light but spicy salad lunch to this hut further down the beach. It was delicious but she drank too much wine. He seemed genuinely surprised when he found out where she worked, but he kept his hands to himself. He told her about Cuba, spoke of politics and food and, gazing at her, of things of beauty. And fast sports cars.

And was dumfounded when he learned that she did not drive.

'You mean you haven't got a car?' he asked her.

'No, I've never even taken driving lessons.'

'Amazing,' he said.

'Well, I'm just an old-fashioned girl, I suppose,' she answered.

When they parted in late afternoon, he had a business appointment he just couldn't put off any longer, he gently kissed her on the cheek. Gallant to a tee. She had expected more. He promised to come and see her at the club very soon.

'You must be a fantastic dancer,' he said. 'I can't wait.'

In fact, Katherine wasn't very good at the dancing thing, really. The other girls working at the joint were all so much better, they had more natural rhythm, the blacks and the Latinas. So, to capture the attention of the men in the audience, she knows she has to offer something different. Not just her amazon build and fair skin and heavy hips. She has shaved her sex, banned the dark curls from between her strong thighs and only kept a thin line of pubic thatch rising straight above the gash, like a small arrow pointing toward her navel. Maria, who helped her do it one evening, had suggested she trim it in the shape of a heart, but Katherine felt that would be quite vulgar and inappropriate. Before every shift, she carefully places a cube of ice over her nipples to render them erect, hard, more prominent, then dries the aroused tips and rouges them with shocking red lipstick. Then, she dips the stick toward her outer labia and colours them beautiful, a fine line on either side delineating the lips, gently separating the geometric poles of her nether opening. She has to remember during her act not to smudge the war paint too much. The other dancers don't like her too much. They think she's a snob, can't really gossip or indulge in silly small talk like they do between sets. She's the first stripper they've come across who spends her time in the dressing room when not on duty actually reading books. By people they've never even heard of. Not your usual Stephen Kings or John Grishams. Thinks she's clever and better than us, does English Eddie, they grumble between themselves.

It's the little extras, Katherine knows, that keep the tips coming. She pouts like other dancers, smiles hypocritically as she sheds the thin items of exotic clothing, sticks out her tongue in pre-orgasmic languor, licks her fingers as she would a penis, bumps and grinds like the best of all sluts, teases the invisible males out there ceaselessly, quickly opening her thighs wide and obscuring the forbidden vista with the palm of her hand, bends over unchastely to reveal the darker band of skin dividing her arse, dances the night and day away, while her mind remains on cruise control, empty of thoughts. She senses the clients in the outlying audience, the smell of man, a quick thrust of her lower stomach forward and there must be one there, no, there, who's jerking off to the sight of her, his hand buried deep inside the trouser pocket, holding his cock in a tight noose as he moves the envelope of his palm and fingers up and down the trunk and comes all over his underwear. She rubs her damp crotch against the small Afghan carpet she now dances on, to avoid splinters in her feet, grinds her lower stomach against the hard floor and a few artificial moans escape as the music quietens momentarily, and somewhere in the back row must be a guy with his dick actually out, rubbing away furiously under a newspaper or a magazine while he drinks in the sheer erotic vision of her and imagines her spread-eagled on some filthy bed while he fucks her like there was no tomorrow. Likely story. Yes, they masturbate, they dream, they drool, and this way, she rationalises, she has power over them.

Control.

Of men.

Like the two left far behind.

At the end of every shift comes the parade.

The house lights come on, the stage lights dim and the dancers stream out and tour the front rows. They are all fully nude. Some of the guys in the audience leave then, while others hurriedly move to the edge of the stage if there is still free space. With their back to the men, the women move from seat to seat, up to a couple of minutes next to each respective guy, words are exchanged, greenbacks change hand and the transaction completed, the stripper either sits on the guy's lap while he paws her breasts until his time is up or alternately stands in close proximity to the punter and allows his hands to wander all over her body. The first two customers say nothing and Katherine moves on to the next seat. The man remains silent, but nods positively. He slips her a couple of crumpled notes. He's old. He rises, he's short, but then most men are compared to her. She moves closer to him, her bust rising gently. He peers at her eyes. His own are watery and vacant. He lowers his hand to her cunt, and swiftly inserts a finger inside her, stretching her dryness.

'Hey!' she exclaims. 'Off limits.'

But the elderly customer fails to respond. They can mangle the dancers' breasts, guessing which are real or silicone-assisted, they can slime over their skin to their heart's content, they can touch, caress, tiptoe like piano-players over the soft bodies, but not down there. His finger moves deeper and Katherine is obliged to open her thighs more to facilitate his intrusion. His nails are scratching her insides. His breath stinks to high heaven. She's about to seize his errant hand to pull it away when the next dancer in line jostles up to her for her turn and the man withdraws and sits down again. Katherine moves on down the flesh parade. It only took a minute or so, or was it more? None of the other men want her, they've had their fill of skin elsewhere already.

It itches like hell inside. She just hopes it's not bleeding from his nails, that he has not infected her. She's an illegal alien, enjoys no medical protection.

Back in the communal dressing room, she grabs a small pocket mirror from her bag and rushes to the toilets. Spreads her thighs open and examines the inside of her vagina. Yes, there's a bad scratch there, but it's not bleeding. She forces herself to pee, to evacuate any foreign elements. She washes herself out thoroughly. When she returns to the backstage area, all the women from her shift have already gone. A couple of dancers from the six pm batch have arrived and are already undressing. Katherine sits herself by one of the make-up mirrors and cleans the lipstick away from her body and slips on a cotton shirt and a pair of loose, baggy shorts. She replaces the mirror in her bag and pulls out her purse to safely put away the meagre notes from the parade. Jesus. Her heart misses a beat. There s no money at all in there. She swears mightily under her breath. A Latina dancer she's never seen here before gives her strange look. One of the girls must have taken it. Could have been any of the women. None of them really liked her. Shit. She had all her cash in there. She can't open a bank account because of her status. Nearly two hundred and twenty dollars, she remembers. How the fuck is she going to settle her bill at the inn tomorrow? Buy groceries. She'd never raise that much in tips in such a short time. Even if she were sheer sex on a stick. Complaining to the elusive club gaffer would be quite useless, she knows.

At the stage door stands Steve. He's now wearing a sharp pale grey suit and she's never seen shoes so shiny. The Miami dusk feels sultry. He smiles at her as she walks out of the joint.

'Hey, you were incredible, Eddie. Are all English girls like you, tell me?'

She answers with a feeble smile and explains what happened.

'Ah, pretty woman, don't worry, it's only money,' he says.

He leads her to his car, parked just outside, a big convertible with shiny metal hubs and metallic green paintwork. He opens a door for her, and she gets in.

'Yeah, but I needed that money, you just don't understand.'

As he settles into the black leather driver's seat and switches on the ignition and the air conditioning starts up with a vengeance, Steve says:

'I know how you can earn a lot of money.'

'When?' Katherine asks.

'Right now, if you wish,' he answers and picks up a cellular phone. The car glides away from the kerb as he begins a long conversation in Spanish. She can't understand a word of course. She'd taken French as her foreign language at the Epsom grammar school. Wasn't even very good at it.

A mile or two down the road, he completes his transaction on the phone.

'All set, honey. For a girl like you, no problem. You see, you re exotic. Good money. Indeed,' he flashes her a broad grin, slips a cassette into the car's system and a raucous beat fills the car, drums and all sorts of wondrous percussion punctuating a joyful Latin tune.

She says nothing but looks at him enquiringly.

'Relax, Eddie, relax, it'll be good. Really good,' he says.

She doesn't like the 'honey', the 'exotic' or the 'relax'. But what are the choices?

A penthouse suite at the Fontainebleau Hotel. A valet has taken the car to be parked. Katherine feels out of place in her shabby casual wear, but Steve reassures her. 'It's not important, Eddie, don't worry.' The lift alone, shiny mirrors and gold-plated knobs everywhere must have cost a million. A long corridor with expensive prints all the way down the walls like a museum or an art gallery. They reach the door. Steve knocks three times. They open.

'This is Eddie,' he introduces her.

There are half a dozen dusky middle-aged businessmen in expensive silk suits that put Steve's garb to shame. This is real money, she recognises. Further back, there is another man, sipping a glass at the huge bar overlooking the balcony. He's black, a giant, must be all of seven feet.

'Meet Orlando, you're from England, aren't you? You won't know him, of course, he's with the 'Gators. One of our local heroes.'

The black guy mumbles something as he weakly shakes her hand.

'A drink, Eddie?' one of the businessmen offers unctuously. 'Absolutely anything you want. A bit of food, we can call room service, if you feel like a snack.' All the guys are watching her attentively. Katherine feels uncomfortable. Never liked hotel rooms since that first time, that Tuesday at the Heathrow hotel when she had for the first time gone over the edge and jettisoned part of her life.

She declines the offer of food, has an ice-cold beer. Dos Equis.

The black guy still stands silently at the bar, looking her over. Most of the businessmen have settled onto chairs and a couple of massive couches. Waiting.

Steve sets his own glass down and comes over to her.

'See, it's like this, Eddie. One thousand dollars. Yes, a whole thousand bucks. My commission is twenty percent. Fair? No?'

She feels her stomach sinking. What's worth all that cash?

'What do I have to do?' she asks.

'A live show. These gentlemen are important business contacts of mine, all the way from South America and down there, they don't have the entertainment we have here in America, so they want to enjoy a real special show.'

A private show. Katherine breathes a sigh of relief. It could have been worse, much worse, she supposes.

'But I left my stage gear at the club,' she points out. 'You should have told me; it's not really sexy with these things I'm wearing now.'

A frown crosses Steve's face.

'Oh, come on, don't be coy, we're not paying this sort of money for a just a strip turn. A live show. Sex. Real sex. Fucking. Here on the bloody carpet, girl, where they can all see it all up close.'

'What...?' she protests.

'With Orlando here,' Steve adds, pointing at the towering sportsman. Absurdly, in her utter confusion, she vainly tries to guess which sport: basket ball, football, baseball? He continues: 'Orlando is a legend. They call him the black stud and my friends wish to see him in action, with a blonde, with very white skin. You. *Comprende?*'

She looks at the black athlete. He is impassive.

'I can't.'

'Yes, you can, bitch, and you will. You re not going to disappoint my friends, are you? Or you'll damn well feel my mighty wrath, woman. Don't disappoint me,' he threatens her. She swallows hard, gulps down the end of her beer. Steve takes her right arm and leads her to the geographical centre of the room, all the businessmen sitting in a circle of sorts around the spot, none of them more than ten or at most twelve feet away. Yes, they would have a good view. Full cinerama widescreen gynaecology in close-up. Better than IMAX.

'Okay, come on, now,' Steve says brusquely.

She keeps on standing there, hesitant.

He is becoming increasingly irritated.

'Eddie, I'm losing patience.'

He suddenly takes hold of her shirt and pulls it open. Reluctantly, she takes it off.

The men all smile.

'Orlando, she's all yours. Let's see that famous big black dick at work,' Steve says excitedly. 'Ride the white bitch. Ride her.'

She unbuttons the shorts and slides them down her hips and legs. Her black knickers haven't been washed for a few days. There's a small hole on one side. She blushes, bends and with her back to the ring of businessmen, takes them off. She looks up. Orlando is already down to his underpants. His chest is quite hairless, the colour of ebony. He wets his lips as his gaze explores her exposed body. The bulge in his crotch rises slightly as he catches sight of her shaven sex. She places her hands needlessly in front.

He extricates his cock from the pants.

It dangles out against his taut thigh.

'Jesus Christ,' she says.

His penis, still soft and unaroused, is enormous. Like a donkey, she thinks. I can never take that inside. It'll rip me apart. He faces her, a few inches away from her. She shivers. His thing down there is like a stick of wood, heavily veined, delicately textured. She smells the man, his odour is strong, fierce. She accumulates saliva at the back of her mouth and swallows it down.

'Suck him, make him grow, ' a voice says in the background, outside of the circle of light in which she feels imprisoned.

She kneels down, touches Orlando's cock. Lifts the shaft to her dry lips. Underneath she sees the heavy sack of his balls, the lined thin skin holding the heavy testicles, the bulging scrotum. She approaches her mouth. She can feel his member throbbing as she holds it. It's growing already. Her tongue emerges and reaches the tip of his glans. He has no foreskin. She closes her eyes and moves her head, her mouth forward. The cock slides between her lips, brushes against her teeth and, pulsing all the time, lodges itself against the back of her throat. She almost chokes and has to adjust her position, raising her head slightly, still the sportsman's penis grows until she feels her whole mouth full, invaded. Her tongue moves around the thick shaft, licking, caressing, tasting the man.

'See, it fits,' she hears Steve, commenting. 'I told you she was a big girl. Look at that ass, the butt of a queen, truly.'

She sucks and sucks to little emotional reaction from the black giant. She's afraid he will come in her mouth, literally drown her throat with his semen, choke her to death. Right then, he places a hand on her freckled shoulder and says: 'I'm ready, girl, now.' And pulls his cock out of her aching mouth.

The massive member stands tall, an inch away from her face. She finally opens her eyes. She's never seen a cock so big, so thick, so long. No, she mentally protests, it'll kill me. It'll never go in. It's physically impossible. It stands at attention, rigid and hard, like a lethal weapon.

She turns around. Steve and half the men have got their cocks out or trousers down. They all seem incredibly thin and long.

'He's got to wear a condom,' she protests.

'No,' says one of the men.

Katherine stands firm.

'Then I can't go along with it, I just can't,' she says. It's possibly her out.

'For a thousand bucks, you'll do what we say,' Steve screams at her. 'This ain't no government health education advertorial.'

He walks over to her and suddenly punches her in the stomach. She bends forward, not so much in pain, but out of breath.

'There, that's a gentle warning.' He pushes her head down to the floor, 'Okay, black stud, poke her. First, turn her over so we've a good view.'

Orlando moves her body round, spits into his palm, wets his cock and positions his raised dick right by her opening. Katherine is on all fours, rump raised to his level, he pulls her hips up and she almost loses balance. She feels the tip of the cock brushing hard against her outer lips. The black man thrusts hard and the glans enters and jams, only partly embedded inside her. Her muscles already feel so stretched, she squirms. Her involuntary movement loosens the inner labia and the main shaft moves an inch forward. It hurts. Bad. His large hands seize her rump as he pushes again.

Two of the men are betting.

'It'll never go in.'

'Yes, it will. She can take him. Hey, Steve, the stud needs some lubrication, help him out.'

She hears him move close and feels a cold liquid pouring down over her ass and into the vaginal gash, pearling over the black cock. Champagne. Orlando grunts, thrusts hard, his hips dictating the sharp movement, the shaft moves further up her cunt. How much more? She moans. Tears are coming to her eyes. One final shove and he is finally all in, she is tearing, she is being cut in two. The black man begins to move inside her, the top of his cock feels as if it's moved so far it's inside her stomach, scraping manically against her inside walls. The movement increases and she blanks out her mind, the pain down there now feels like an anaesthetic, remote, someone else's. Eternity and over.

'Great ass, hey. Love that mole under the left butt, or is it a beauty spot?' Steve remarks from his vantage point.

White on black.

Black cock inside white cunt.

'Turn over,' one of the men says. 'Missionary, now.'

Orlando disengages. It feels like a hole inside her. He pulls her over and down, settles her shoulders and the back of her head on the carpet. She looks down her body. She is gaping open. She gasps, it'll never close up again. The outer lips are redder than they were with all the lipstick. The black sportsman, with his cock still at full mast kneels down and with one hand moves the cock back into her. He bobs up and down over her, as the dick slides in and out until it reaches port and impales her totally. Then he pulls her legs up and places them over his own shoulders, still thrusting savagely inside her all the time. For the first time, she feels an early wave of pleasure run through her. Her nipples are so sensitive. Why doesn't Orlando touch them? Please. Her lover did. The black man's breath grows shorter. She senses his climax approaching as his eyes open and close in quick succession as he pistons on inside her, his big balls slamming like a metronome against her bum.

'Hey,' Steve shouts out. 'Orlando, my man, don't come inside her. Let's see your spunk on her face.'

The stud digs ever deep into her. Vaginal farts punctuate his movements as the air left inside her is displaced by his sheer bulk. Finally, he pulls out hurriedly and his come spurts out like a geyser, white, creamy, burning hot over her shaven mons and her thighs.

'He missed the target,' one of the joker says.

The black guy, spent, looks Katherine in the eyes. 'Sorry,' he whispers. 'I needed the money too. Gambling debts.'

He walks away, standing tall, to fetch his clothes.

Quarter of an hour later. Orlando has left and all the businessmen have had another round of drinks. Katherine is still spread out on the thick carpet of the hotel suite, aching madly, her legs still obscenely apart, the lips of her sex still unnaturally dilated, it still hurts too much to close her thighs and steal her live porno movie away from the men.

'So, gentlemen,' Steve says. 'Good show, hey? Nothing beats a big, strong blonde. Any of you want a sample now? Please yourselves. No extra cost.'

How can he, Katherine mutters?

The South Americans confer between themselves. Finally, one of them says: 'Thanks, but no thanks, compadre. That pussy's been used up for today. I'd float in there. I don't care about the black guy, they're all bloody animals, but I don't know where that pussy's been before. I've a family, you know. Get rid of her.'

Steve pulls her up. She staggers across the room. He slips her an envelope, together with her crumpled clothes.

'It's all there. Now you can nicely bugger off, Eddie. And don't even think of ever mentioning this to anyone or I'll cut you up so badly your mother wouldn't recognise you. Understood?'

He opens the door and pushes her out into the corridor.

She's quite naked, she knows she looks a real mess, the black stud's spunk is still seeping out somehow between her lower lips, or is it some sort of personal secretion? There s a bad bruise on the inside of her thigh.

As he closes the door:

'I'd slip something on pronto, girl, if I were you. There might be a hotel detective on the prowl,' he laughs.

She hurriedly dresses and makes her way to the lifts. Yes, her lover had once said, I will celebrate you like no man has ever done, Kate. Yes, all the things he would say as his fingers kept lingering in the small of her back after the act of love.

She's travelled to Las Vegas. Another stage of her American kaleidoscope. She'd remembered someone once saying how cheap the food and hotels happened to be, subsidised as they were by all the gambling. One of her directors had been there for a bookselling convention, and mentioned the fact. Like a modern Jack Kerouac heroine she'd made the journey on Greyhound buses, crisscrossing the vast plains and their surrounding roadside galleries of decrepit motels and gas stations. And then, one morning at dawn, racing out of the desert into the garish canyons of light of Vegas, she had come across her new, temporary home.

She found a small residential hotel at an unfashionable end of the Strip, where the gamblers never went and working class families with kids, mostly from Jersey, stayed. She even managed to bargain down the weekly rate. She avoided the big casinos and the glittering joints. Not again. She tried to get waitressing jobs, but they all said she was too old. Did they mean unattractive, she wondered? Here, most of the women were icily perfect. Surgically designed to appeal to the average American male. Frosty lipstick, eye shadow galore, tight skirts, no visible panty line. Not quite her.

After costing her room and the steak breakfast specials ever on offer all around, Katherine estimated she could last a whole month before she would run out of cash. I need a holiday, anyway, she thought.

She often walked out to the desert when night fell, to breathe in the pure, dry air. She grew to recognise all the amazing species of cacti growing in the wilderness that surrounded the town. The night sky was so amazingly clear. If only she could remember which constellations were which from her wasted school days. The heavens were a subtle tapestry of lights, delicately enhanced by the reddish glow of the electric city illuminating the surrounding mountains.

Less than a year ago when she and her husband had moved into their new mews house, before all hell broke loose over her affair, she had intended to fulfil an earlier ambition and begin writing stories in earnest. She'd finally have a study, a space of her own. Nothing had come of it. Life had conspired to thwart her again.

Now was the time, Katherine decided, buying a yellow legal

pad.

The story begins.

'My husband is a good man. My husband is a gentle man. Even though the passing of the years has hardened him and he is no longer the young man with whom I shared my early student poverty, he is still the man I sleep with. I smell his stale breath when he awakes in the morning and it does not offend me. I see the faint stains in his underwear before I load up the washing machine and it doesn't shock or disgust me. My marriage is the most important thing in my life. I treasure it. I protect it from the storms. I shield myself behind it. I've messed up so many other things, but my marriage will survive against the odds and divorce statistics. It will work. It must work.

'My husband and I argue a lot. He cries when we go to sentimental films, while my eyes remain dry. I have a cold heart, you see. I'm not romantic. I don't know why. The way I was brought up, I suppose. We've lived together seven years, married for five of them. Two flats. One house. No children. My husband wants us to have babies, and he is becoming more insistent. Soon I shall turn thirty; I mustn't leave it too late, he says. I don't want kids right now, I tell him but what I mean is that I don't want kids at all. I don't like the way adults go all soft and mushy in the presence of babies; children get on my nerves, they cry, they show off, they are loud. I would be a bad mother.

'Once I could have justified my actions by invoking my career, my brilliant career. Now I can no longer do so. People think I have a prestigious job, but it's not what I thought it would be. There are too many frustrations. So, I am left with much emptiness.

'The lovemaking is not what it used to be. We're growing older together. Too familiar with each other. All too often, at night, he is tired and falls asleep without even finishing reading the financial papers. He is ambitious, has lofty aspirations for his own career. Works hard. Some times, in the morning, he feels randy and arranges his body against mine, presses himself against my back, rubs his cock against my arse, lazily fingers my breasts. I wet my fingers and lubricate my opening and manually insert him. On most occasions he's only half-erect. He screws me in utter silence. I like being taken from behind. It makes me feel more sensitive. Our morning fucks barely scratch the itch in my guts. Oh, there's nothing bad about it. I'm sure most other couples are no more animated or passionate than we are. Once or twice a year, he whizzes me off to a small country hotel for a long week-end. The lovemaking is better. I even orgasm sometimes. But in the mornings, it's always over too fast. He comes inside me and my thighs are all damp as he pulls out and rushes to the bathroom. He only has a half hour left to shave, wash, dress, eat before he leaves for the studio or the outside broadcast he's been assigned to. But, all in all, he is a good, kind man, my husband. He forgives my trespasses. Tolerates my wild, irrational tempers. The tall man I married for better or for worse.'

She put her pen down. Enough for today.

She takes a coach and visits the Hoover Dam, one hour's drive out of Vegas.

The view is majestic. The vast expanse of water in the lake is utterly surreal in this desert environment. She journeys down with visiting crowds to the bottom of the dam, to the heart of the concrete monster and feels quite dwarfed by the sheer power of the construction. At the end of the tour, she goes to the cafeteria with its huge bay windows at water level and sits herself down with a coffee and a sticky cake. A man accosts her. Identifying his accent is easy. He's Welsh. Works in local government or education, it doesn't quite register with her. But it's nice not to have to communicate with yet another Yank. He's here with a group of friends. Fellow professionals, he insists. Enjoying a spot of gambling. They're having a small party and card game in their room at the Mirage tonight. Yes, the Casino with the live volcano outside. Would she like to join them? She must be homesick, surely. It would be nice to hear more normal accents. Two of the boys are from Bristol, he tells her.

Once in the room, she first notices the other woman. Auburn hair, round face, dark glasses, black halter top and tight white jeans. The other men, the Brits, seem unappealing. More like lager louts on a sun, booze and sex holiday to Ibiza. Her host, is name is Maurice, effects the introductions. She quickly forgets the men's names. Two of them are junior doctors and the third one a sales executive, a rep for a pharmaceutical company who's probably picking up the bill. The woman's name is Vicky.

'It's not my real name,' she tells Katherine when she joins her in the bathroom where they powder their nose and cheeks. 'It was Liliana, but it was wrong. I just don't feel like a Lily or a Liliana, really. So I changed it.'

She is American, from Phoenix, Arizona, has been in Vegas six months now, some waitressing, some hosting, a personal escort agency had found her tonight's gig. 'Very respectable, classy, you know, they actually advertise in the local papers. So you're English too? Who do you work for?' she asks.

'I don't,' Katherine answers. 'Freelance,' she explains. Why complicate matters? She knows all to well why she has been invited here tonight. Fresh meat. Orifices.

There are dark shadows under Vicky's eyes. Her face is heavily freckled and the freckles continue all the way down her front and disappear inside her cleavage. Her neck is intensely pale. She wears her hair up in a delicately sculpted bun. She is quite small and delicate and once must have been ever so pretty, baby-faced until time finally caught up with her. Her eyes, once the sunglasses come off, are revealed to be dark green. Hypnotic. Under the halter top, she has medium-sized breasts, Katherine sees, as Vicky lifts the material to powder her tits. A reflection catches her eye in the mirror. Katherine can't stop herself staring at the other woman's breasts. They are so round. Almost perfect. Pierced. She's even a touch envious of both these impeccably rounded orbs and the striking adornments. She'd never have the guts. She used to faint at the dentist's.

'You're very pretty,' she tells the other woman.

'Thanks, dear.' She readjusts her top, wriggles her bum inside the tight jeans. 'Shall we? Your English buddies are waiting for their entertainment.'

The men ply the girls with drinks. The ensuing conversation is rowdy, suggestive but innocent enough to begin with. Maurice, who seems in charge of orchestrating the proceedings, is particularly boisterous, and his jokes are actually on occasion witty. They order snacks from room service, and the obligatory champagne. Katherine relaxes. Gazes at the men. Tries to imagine what they would all look like in their birthday suits. That one must have a hairy chest, what about the beer belly on the other one, another must surely have a big cock, don't like the last one though, looks a bit evil.

'Well, boys, this is Vegas. Time to gamble. What's your poison?' Maurice asks.

'Poker.'

'Strip poker.'

They all giggle and look toward the two women sipping their drinks on the mustard couch.

The pharmaceutical rep devises an infinitely complex set of rules for the game, to ensure they all shed clothing fast enough, including Katherine and Vicky, who are assigned to respective card players.

They play.

Vicky is the first to end up unclothed. Katherine still has her underwear on. And garter belt and stockings. She knows from experience how much men like her when she wears them. The carousing Brits are soon all shirtless, one is down to his jockey shorts.

The American woman has a small, compact body, her legs are not that great, and sports two thick gold rings on her nipples. Adorned à la modern primitive. The rings glisten inside the pierced puckered, dark red skin of the nipples. Katherine can't disguise her intense fascination. As are the guys; their tongues almost sticking out when they catch sight of Vicky's extraordinary boobs and their unnatural metal extensions. One of the medics deliberately loses his next hand to carry Vicky to the next stage where forfeits begin.

'She has to play with her tits,' one of them orders.

Vicky does.

She twists the darker skin between her nimble fingers, pulls the tips of her round breasts through the hoops of the rings, distends the flesh to impossible proportions. Asks the man nearest to her to lick her fingers and then smears the moist secretion over her abnormally erect nipples. They are all entranced. Katherine included.

Vicky tires of manipulating herself. 'Next round,' she says.

Inevitably, all the clothing is shed. The men sit there around the table, self-conscious, exchanging nervous glances at each other, a couple of them are semi-erect, another handles himself but fails to harden his stem; too much drink.

'Isn't this great?' Maurice exclaims to break the silence. 'More champagne, ladies and gentlemen.' He stands up to get the last bottle from the room service trolley. He has a fat, floppy arse.

He brushes past Katherine as he pours the drink for her and, with his free hand, roughly fondles her left breast. She finds it, and him, deeply unpleasant and shivers. He ignores her reaction.

The women are now excluded from the card game and the men play between themselves for forfeits. Katherine looks over at Vicky. The auburn-haired woman has settled back on the couch, her legs wide open in a truly indecent posture. She joins her, thighs together, more demure. She can't stop herself looking down at Vicky's bush where she notices a thin line of secretions separating her cunt lips. Vicky notices her gaze. The inner juice seeps into the thick rust-coloured vegetation.

'I'm a bit excited,' she confesses. She's a bit drunk. 'I hope they ask us to do it together first,' she says.

Katherine bites her tongue. She's never had any kind of sexual contact with a woman before. Well, there was this girl, Diane, back at grammar school. When they showered after hockey one day, Katherine had once blushed to her roots when she had been caught daydreaming and staring at the other girl's budding breasts and the first growth of thin hair on her pubis. She looks into Vicky's green eyes. She has an uncomfortable feeling in the pit of her stomach. On the other hand, she's getting wet, inside. Anticipation?

Inevitably, British males have so little imagination, that's what the guys ask for.

Vicky takes Katherine's hand and leads her to the carpet. The men settle in their chairs, pulling them away from the card table, idly fingering their cocks.

She gently pushes Katherine down, her back against the floor. She slides back, parts Katherine's thighs, opens her legs wide and moves her head towards the beckoning crotch. She licks the shaven lips, and a jolt of raw electricity runs through Katherine's body. Jesus. Vicky gnaws at the entrance and soon inserts her tongue inside the now dripping vagina. The men have grown totally silent. The agile, experienced tongue moves in as deep as she can manage it. Katherine closes her eyes. The warm, velvety, darting tongue then moves upwards and envelops her clitoris. Katherine can feel the bud swelling. She can no longer control her body and a spasm races across her stomach. The tongue deftly extracts the expanding clitoris from its thin hood and Vicky moves her head forward slightly so that her teeth are now chewing Katherine's button. Jesus. Jesus. She sighs. He used to do it exactly the same way. But the American woman quickly tires and now uses two fingers to frig Katherine off. As she does so distractedly, she whispers:

'You taste really nice.'

Katherine looks down at the auburn bun bobbing up and down between her thighs and the jerky movement of the hand ending up inside her, stimulating her inner parts with knowing cunning and talent. The pleasure moves up and up through her.

'69?' Vicky suggests.

She circles Katherine's body and lowers her own, hairy dark cunt over Katherine's face as she lies down on her, stomach to stomach, breasts almost joined, slightly out of alignment. She licks away at her cunt again in the new position and Katherine timidly extends her tongue upward where it loses itself in the woman's thick, curly bush. She has to use her fingers to find a way through the pubic hair, separates Vicky's cunt leaves and slips her tongue inside the other woman.

She tastes so strong. Katherine almost gags initially, but overcomes her reluctance and begins licking the inner walls opening up above her. Vicky is a prolific secreter and soon her juices are flooding Katherine's mouth, settling in a ring around her mouth, pungent, an abundant gluey deposit.

'Wow,' says one the men.

Soon, Katherine finds a rhythm and her tongue patterns its in-and-out intrusions against the movement of Vicky's head and mouth lower down. It even settles into a routine. She feels the heat increasing in her throat and lungs. She must be so wet down there too. It's both repugnant and perversely pleasing. She wonders if men really enjoy it.

A hand strokes her damp forehead. She opens her eyes again. It's one of the men.

'Oh, it's a waste of talent,' another says. 'Now for the real stuff.'

Yet another walks over as Vicky disengages herself and Katherine is left sprawled, open, spread-eagled on the carpet as the men surround the two women.

Passively, Katherine and Vicky allow the men to position them, next to each other, on all fours as two move to the front and insert their cocks into the women s mouths and the remaining two fuck them doggie-style from behind. The cock in Katherine's mouth is flaccid, and all her best efforts fail to raise it from the dead. In her rear, Maurice pistons away, punctuating his thrusts with hard slaps on her rump. He withdraws, and exchanges positions with the medic who'd been screwing Vicky. The new cock plunges into her still dilated opening, and the guy quickly comes. In her mouth, the useless cock is just another piece of meat. The third man removes himself from Vicky's mouth as Maurice, still hard, keeps on screwing the American woman relentlessly and positions himself behind her. The plump man's labouring instrument is very thick and painfully stretches her cunt muscles. However, he ejaculates quickly, and Katherine feels her innards drowning in the mixed come of the two men. The man in her mouth still labours on, to no avail.

'Hey, not there,' Vicky screams, next to her. Katherine turns her head but cannot see what Vicky is complaining about to Maurice, or the other man. She's no longer sure who is doing what to who.

After all the fun and games are over, the two women wash themselves out in the adjoining bathroom. Katherine watches the men's seed mingle in the tub with the soapy water, as it seeps, on and on from her body as she squats over the bath.

'Well, that was quite fun,' Vicky remarks, adjusting her make-up in front of the bathroom mirror.

They leave the Mirage together and become friends. But they never have sex together again. 'I prefer men,' Vicky tells her one morning when Katherine, curious, questions her. 'Anyway, your heart wasn't in it. You're not truly bi.'

When the cash runs out, Vicky helps her get a job in a peep show on the wrong side of town, where she herself does the occasional shift when funds are short. The money's good and the security guys see to it that there's no funny business. Six hours a day, Katherine sits in a cubicle in diaphanous lingerie, while men open the door to enter the other side of the closet, a glass window separating them. There is a telephone to communicate between the two areas. For five dollars, the men get three minutes during which she strips and follows their utterly predictable instructions. They are without surprises. They ask her to touch herself. Breasts. Pussy. Sometimes even feet. For an extra ten dollars, which they can insert through a hand-sized aperture in the glass partition, she will spread her legs wide and open her pussy to their gaze; for an extra twenty, she will even insert a flesh-coloured dildo inside her cunt and pretend to masturbate. Invariably, they all lower their trousers to jerk off. An attendant has to wipe the come off the glass partition and sweep the floor with disinfectant every fifteen minutes or so. When rent day approaches, Vicky teaches her a new trick, which is strictly speaking not allowed, but where the management operate a blind eye policy. For another fifty dollars, she will also allow the guy to thread his hand through the opening and paw her. One day, one man goes too far and scratches her badly. Katherine gives up the job and packs her meagre belongings. There are too many books, all used, read a few times each already, too much to carry. Vicky says she'll join her. They leave Las Vegas and head for the Coast.

Katherine is waitressing at the bar of a big hotel near LAX. Randy businessmen make half-hearted passes, but don't seem too disappointed when she politely turns them down. She's not the Angeleno type. The tips aren't too good and the hours are long and awkward. She still lives with Vicky; they share a small apartment in a block near Pacific Palisades. Vicky sometimes disappears for days on end. Katherine never asks where she has been. There are often marks on her body. One morning as she surprises her in the shower, Katherine sees that the small American woman now sports a snake tattoo weaving its way down from her navel to her bush. Christ, that must have been fucking painful, she thinks. Another time, she sees a bad scar on Vicky's rump. Deliberate. Burnt into the flesh. They are seldom together at the apartment anymore. Waitressing and sex work hours seldom coincide.

It's Katherine's day off. Big plans for today; she's going to lounge by the communal pool and finally start Proust. She's been putting it off for years. And next, she's planning on Dostoevsky. She's always been meaning to fill these gaps in her literary culture.

She lies in bed, vaguely daydreaming as always of the men she has left behind. Does she still love, miss, think of them? She just doesn't know any longer. Vicky walks in. She looks rough.

'Hi, Kate? Got the day off, hey?'

'Yes.'

'Listen. I badly need a favour,' she says. 'I'm feeling damn rotten. My period has started and I'm in pain all over. But I've been paid in advance for a job today. Can you go there instead?'

'What sort?' Katherine enquires.

'A film.'

'Nudity?' Katherine asks.

'Yeah, of course. But if you ask, they won't show your face. There are lotsa other girls involved, so they won't mind.'

Vicky runs to the bathroom where she is promptly sick. She returns, awfully pale and tense. She nervously insists. 'Please, I just can't face it today. Be a pal. Please.'

Katherine acquiesces. She's stripped before. Never before a camera, though. And she likes Vicky in a quiet, affectionate way.

Vicky books a cab for the afternoon. It's a villa in the Hollywood Hills. She bargains with the producers.

'It's all fixed. He even said that if you're real glamourous, you could get a bonus. I told him you're incredibly tall and have wild hair. He was very excited. You'll have to doll yourself up a bit. Here, ' she extracts a note from her handbag. 'Fifty bucks, buy yourself something special at the mall, something nice. You English gals have so much taste.'

Katherine spends it all, and more, at Victoria's Secret, where the lingerie is supposed to be English but comes from somewhere in Ohio or thereabouts, she read in a magazine. The underwear is slinky, the silk glistens, she knows how easily she could become a serious silk fetishist with stuff like this. She could spend a fortune on underwear alone. A black slip that adheres to her body through the sheer force of gravity, a pair of knickers, more like a thong, the sheer fabric dissecting her bum cheeks and enhancing the drop of her wide hips. A brassiere that hooks up at the back like a corset. Stockings as soft as flesh. In the cubicle, she looks at her body in the mirror. She feels the onset of wetness between her thighs. God, I'm such a slut.

The villa has white walls, most of the furniture has been moved out the main room, and its windows open up on a large pool outside. They're already filming there when she arrives. A brassy, artificial blonde stands inside, the water lapping around her waist, her breasts are large and unnatural. A silicone job, no doubt. A tubby guy sits on the edge and she is sucking his cock with a distinct lack of enthusiasm, while the camera peers into the action in close-up. The cameraman is incredibly hairy and wears only Bermuda shorts. Out of camera range, two other couples lounge around, some nude, others with towels around their waist. She recognises one of the men. It's Steve; Esteban, from Miami.

He sees and waves.

'Hey, if it isn't English Eddie?'

She acknowledges his presence with a silent gesture.

The peroxide blonde in the pool changes position with the man and he starts sucking on her genitals, once the cameraman has changed his film. Her pubes are also peroxide blonde. The straw yellow patch seems so damn wrong. A young guy, who looks more like a student, but is actually the director, shouts out:

'Come on, give it some more life. You're supposed to be enjoying it.'

The porno actor ignores him and chews away impassively.

Finally, 'Cut. Let's move on to another scene. Everybody's here. The whole cast. Orgy time, kids.'

She's asked to strip. They won't even let her wear the new lingerie. A female assistant powders her thigh to hide a small bruise, then moves on to another one of the women who spreads her thighs open and instructs the gofer to powder over the pimples spreading like a rash around her cunt.

The director orders them to spread out in a daisy chain by the pool side. She's asked to fellate the guy in front of her as he lies on his back and Steve rams her from behind and the peroxide blonde from the previous sequence licks out his arsehole and fingers his balls while he moves in and out of Katherine.

One fleeting moment, she imagines her husband out on the town with a group of other journalists and friends, maybe tomorrow his brother the architect is getting married; they have a meal in Chinatown, cruise the pubs getting increasingly drunker and land in some Soho film club to watch dirty movies. He recognises her cunt, and is sick as he is forced to watch the alien penis invade her private sanctum in larger than life dimensions. Which is how he must have felt when he had learned of her cheating. The hurt.

Steve pumps away, whispers:

'Fancy meeting like this again, lady. Destiny, I'm sure.'

The director has them change positions.

Now a small redhead is asked to eat her out while Steve's long, thin member invests her mouth and forces its way almost down her throat. Another's hand roughly manipulates her nipples, twisting, pulling, squeezing between sharp nails. She can't see anything. The strong lights blind her and all she can hear is the monotonous whirr of the nearby camera's motor as it captures the scene and her infamy forever. The redhead isn't very good. She has a small bald patch and a birthmark on her back, like a map of Italy. Her aroma is distinctive. Do all redheads smell this way?

Behind her, she hears one of the guys cry out that he's coming, and the cameraman rushes off to catch the moment; the man's momentary partner fakes aural orgasm. Katherine tastes the pre-ejaculate filtering from the tip of the Cuban's cock shortly before he withdraws. The sparky assistant brings them all cool drinks and they move inside the villa.

The women don't speak to each other as they troop in. The men follow. The tubby one has lost his erection. As the next camera set-up is prepared, he strokes himself to regain his rigidity. It doesn't work. The director asks the girls to help him out.

'I don't do that,' the redhead says.

The peroxide blonde says:

'He smells. At the pool was enough.'

Katherine lowers her eyes when the young director looks in her direction.

'Okay, Okay already,' he calls the young assistant over. 'Hey, Markie, this is what they taught you at film school, no? Help the poor guy out.'

'You bastard,' the all-purpose assistant answers, but moves over to the temporarily impotent actor and takes hold of his cock as she lowers her mouth toward it. 'Better not film any of this.'

Soon, the actor is functional again.

He's instructed to mount Katherine in the missionary position while the others adopt a variety of lovemaking positions around them. He squeezes himself inside her and quickly loses his hardness. They're filming the others. He moves ever so slightly inside her so as not to slip out. He winks at her. She's quite happy to keep on pretending. This goes on forever, and no one notices their lack of ardour as the other couples make up in noise and movement for the faking couple.

'Cut. You can all rest a bit now. Steve,' the director calls over to him. 'You seem fresh. In better shape than the other guys. Okay, you and curly hair here, let's do the anal.'

The others walk away to the pool.

Katherine suddenly realises what comes next.

'No, no, I can't do that,' she says, pleadingly, to the men, the young whey-faced director, the aggressively erect Steve and the sweating cameraman.

'Love,' the director says. 'It's part of the deal. Every hardcore movie has anals now. That's what the guys want. Don't tell me you've never done one. Everyone in the business has to. It's the money shot.'

'I won't come inside you,' Steve adds. 'When the time comes, I'll pull out and do a facial, Okay?'

The cameraman signifies his assent.

'No,' Katherine timidly pleads one last time.

Steve takes hold of her wrist and twists it hard.

'Eddie,' he says, 'you're a bit of a tease, aren't you. I remember the last time, you like to play hard to get, hey; you always have cold feet, don't you?'

Markie the assistant comes over as they set Katherine down on her stomach and help her raise her rump so that the camera can catch it all. They adjust the lights. Shine the warm spots on her utterly exposed rear. Markie carefully sponges Katherine's genitals and between her cheeks, to clean the perspiration away and then gently pours some oil around her anal aperture as well as Steve's penis still standing at attention.

Katherine closes her eyes. She's never been entered there. Penetrated. Fucked. Sodomised. But, she remembers all those nights lying in silence next to her sleeping, cuckolded husband, her whole body consumed by the thoughts of transgression. Her lover had soon discovered how sensitive she was down there and they had often speculated about it. Sometime after they had split up and he was writing her these desperate letters to get her back, change her mind, he had revealed that for weeks he had kept some butter in the fridge in his office for that very purpose.

The cameraman adjusts his focus.

'Filming.'

Steve inserts one finger inside her to spread the oil around. With his other hand, he parts her arse cheeks as wide as he can and places his hard cock against the puckered opening. Initial pressure, the sphincter muscles resist and he makes no headway. He grabs his stem and holding it in a tight vice manually begins to spear her anus. The head moves an inch or so past the outer ring. It feels like constipation backwards. She clenches her teeth. The lubrication takes effect and with one swift move the head inserts itself. Katherine hold her breath.

'Yeah, nice and slow,' the cameraman, or is it the director, says.

She's tearing, she knows it. Her opening is being sundered. Literally split apart. She's often fingered herself there, but this is like a knife, a pole, a gun.

Steve thrusts his hips and breaks through. The cock savagely tears in and impales her to the hilt.

Katherine screams.

This is worse than anything ever. She wants to faint, die, make it all go away. Her whole soul seems focused on the opening to her arse where the long, thin cock is planted. Steve ceases all movement. She senses the cock still growing inside her, her inner walls being forcibly pushed further and further back.

'Focus closer. Now. Now.'

The man initiates a steady movement, a quick coming and going inside her guts. To her utter shame, Katherine feels an odious sort of pleasure, excitement radiating out from her forced aperture down to her cunt, up through her stomach. Her heart falters. The movements increase. Every reverse movement of the cock a few inches out of her hole pulls the inner flesh out, the tight, textured pink private flesh sticking like glue to the dark thrusting cock, and then back in again. Secretions accelerate, coat the moving penis trunk in a ring of white thin cream.

'Hey, she looks good,' another male voice explains. The others have come in from the pool to watch the action.

'Yes,' says Steve, between regular thrusts. 'She has the perfect butt for anal. Great fit, man.'

The other man is in front of the kneeling Katherine. She looks up. He's growing erect, his pole rising steadily as he keeps on watching the Cuban digging into her depths in a metronomic movement, and her head shaking forward with every thrust.

'What about a DP, man?' the voyeur asks the director.

'Good idea,' he says.

Katherine's mouth is so dry. She gasps for breath.

'Look, she's all flushed,' the other man says.

Katherine's face and chest have gone a deep shade of pink. Like a stain racing across her body, as the orgasm approaches, stronger than anything before. The cock in her arse still keeps on moving deeper, seemingly labouring her intestines, she wills it further, her inner muscles gripping the hard tool, sucking it in a vampiric embrace.

Steve slows down, pulls her back slightly, still carefully lodged in her rectum and the other porno actor slides down on his back and moves under her raised upper body. She can feel her sweat raining down over him. He slithers into position and positions his raised cock under her sex lips. She feels the wetness shamefully dripping from her cunt onto his glans and he inserts himself.

'Jesus, Jesus, Jeezus...'

Both men are now fucking her.

They move in unison. As one thrusts, another retreats to the edge of his respective opening. Fire races through her. Her mind is on fever. They now coordinate their movements and thrust inside her together. The cocks rub against her inner walls, teasing each other through the thin layer of skin separating them. She imagines the vision of her double penetration on the cinema screen: the two inhumanly large cocks tearing her pale, white skin in two, digging ever deeper holes, the inhumanly dilated ringed anus as one pulls back, the gaping vaginal gash open like a flower of desire as the foreign object buries itself inside her ever-accommodating cunt. Her husband and her lover watching, both masturbating away. This is me, this is me, she says.

'I'm running out of film,' the cameraman says. 'We need the come shot.'

The two men withdraw violently, wrenching her guts, take hold of their cocks and pump away manually at speed and come. Over her. Her face. Her rump.

'Lick it,' the director says.

Her tongue moves across her lips, tastes the salty emissions, it sticks in the back of her throat when she tries to swallow.

'Good show, Eddie,' Steve says, smearing his come all over her smooth back side. 'We should do it again, in private, you know. I can teach you some more tricks.'

The other women quickly expedite another sequence where they gluttonously eat each other out for the length of another roll of film. Katherine rests. Sips several cans of beer. It grows dark outside. All the actors are growing tired.

'I've got another few minutes of film left,' the cameraman points out. 'Waste not, want not. Anything we haven't got in the can yet?'

Steve says to the director: 'Do you want to try and do something different? I've only seen it done once, you know, by Cameo, a double cuntal.'

'That would be good,' the young man says. 'Who?'

'I'll do it,' Katherine says.

The positioning is awkward. It's not painful; since the black guy in Vegas, she knows she can take any size. And by now, neither of them can stay fully hard. They clumsily do the act. One of the cocks keeps slipping out. Neither men feels the friction of the two pricks against each other inside her very stimulating. Ten minutes is all it takes. They might salvage two minutes in the edit.

Cut.

That night, she writes again in the yellow legal pad.

'My lover is a pornographer. My lover writes vile stories in which he degrades me. I am always amazed by how white his eyes are, peering into mine as he moves inside my body. He has dark curls on his chest and whispers dirty words in my ear when we are engaged in the act of love, making wild promises he will never keep of all the cities and places he will one day take me to. My wild lover whose hair never stands still says he no longer wants to share me. He betrays our original agreement and scares me deeply. He is unpredictable. I never know what he will say or do next. To me. To my ignorant husband.

'When my lover loves me he positions me on the bed or, more often because of the unfortunate nature of our clandestine encounters, on the floor. He cups his hands under my bum, and raises it slightly while his mouth approaches me. He parts my lower lips with gentle, loving care, brushing my moist curls back and kisses the outer folds of my sex. He takes his time. He does not hurry. He teases my senses like an expert. He knows every inch of my body and trips the light fandango all over. He divides my sex into dozens of distinct areas and knows the right word and touch for each. Mons. Outer labia. Inner labia. Folds. Bud. Hood. Walls. Vagina. Cervix. Spots all the way from A to G. Where did he learn all this? Watching porno movies, he says. His tongue moves inside me and he takes my clitoris, the small bud, in between his lips. He chews, he licks, he sucks and bites it and the inside of my cunt. He tastes my most intimate secretions and never protests. I know I smell down there. He sniffs me and smiles. He perspires and I drink in his sharp scent. Until I cry enough, I want you inside me now. And his thick, dark cock plunges into me. Chews my ear lobe. Licks the acrid perspiration from my arm pits. He has no shame.

'As he fucks me, my lover inserts a slow finger up my arse, beyond the tiny ridge of flesh that just hangs there like a superfluous growth. We copulate, his finger pushes, slides, swivels, rotates inside me and a warm feeling invades my stomach and I almost pee all over him as we move together convulsively and my head bangs against the bed rest or the office wall.

'After love, we talk. And he frightens me again. We share saté sticks and Tesco dips in the darkness. Once he brings sushi pieces.

'We fuck again. Like animals. Over and again. He never tires. We are sore. I never want to go home.

'The last time I saw my lover, it was pouring and my hair was flat and he held an oversize umbrella to protect himself. I shouted at him, swore. He didn't say much, just handed me this letter he had written and walked away through the drizzle. Peace, is all he asked. How can you, I thought? But my erstwhile lover sometimes has no decency. He is a wild, dark-haired man. My late lover who angers me so much I once almost tried to hire some thug to go and break his legs. I suppose I read too many crime books.'

Her insides ache. She goes to sleep.

A few days later, Katherine almost collapsed with pain while serving behind the hotel bar. The head barman sent her home and she went to see a doctor. She had a bad infection. No doubt someone on that crazy film shoot. At least it wasn't Aids. All the money she had saved had to pay for the necessary antibiotics.

Vicky has gone. One morning, her clothes and belongings were no longer there. On her own, Katherine could not afford the rent.

She looked at her face in the bathroom mirror. Her brown eyes seem dull. She has spots. She took a long bath, soaking in the warmth. The hairs above her crotch are growing back, hard, wiry, the shaving had irritated the skin and she squeezed some yellow pus from a small pimple there.

She packed her clothes in a canvas tote bag, leaving the legal pad on the dresser. She had only managed to write a few pages. E for effort.

Once on the highway, she hitched North to Seattle. Not one driver made a pass at her during the course of her journeys up the coastline.

They seek her here, they seek her there, they seek her everywhere, but Katherine hides her shame among the deep forests of the Pacific Northwest, reaches the Seattle hills and the vast expanses of blue water that surround the city. She takes up smoking. It rains a lot. On clear days, she gazes at Mount Rainier looming over the horizon of the Seattle skyline. On the way here, she has lost most of her clothes, and barely has enough to keep her warm as winter approaches. But she still holds on to the sheer silk lingerie from Victoria's Secret, even though she has no occasion to wear it any longer, living as she does in tight, soiled tee-shirts, an old brown leather waistcoat, a birthday present from her lost husband, and patched-up jeans.

She moves like a white ghost through and beyond the sexual pale.

There's an advertisement in the local free paper. An agency is looking for entertainers. Good pay. Open mind required. The first job she is given is to jump out of a massive cake at a party for a group of Microsoft localising editors celebrating the completion of another software development project. She is given a skimpy outfit, all glitter and vulgarity. She emerges from the hollow cake. They're all so young. Boys really. She steps out and dances on the table top. They holler and cheer like frat boys. She shakes her butt, tweaks her nipples inside the thin fabric of the oversize bra, and then pulls her small tits out to another triumphant roar from the boys. Later, she smears the remnants of the rich cream from the cake all over her body and allows the drunken technicians to lick it off her. Very few actually take advantage of her, barely a tongue or a hand ventures lower down. After she has cleaned up, she joins some of the guys for a friendly drink. They're rather boring. Even here, most can only discuss computer lore. One of the young men stares at her behind thick round glasses. She goes home with him. He's clumsy but gentle and she stays with him for a fortnight. He buys her small cute presents, a teddy bear, a bracelet. Katherine doesn't like cute. He's besotted with her. Gets a small ring, some special alloy that means a lot in computer land, proposes marriage. He doesn't care about her past. Loves her. Will make her happy. It's never an option for Katherine, Martin is kind but he just has no poetry. She leaves his condo without even writing him an explanatory note.

That's what I do to men who worship me. You should have known.

She is used and abused.

In a vacant car lot next to the Egyptian Theatre, she gives blow jobs for just a few bucks. The men come in all shapes and sizes. When they lower their pants or open their flies, she smells the evil in them. They come unwashed, young and old alike. She retracts the foreskins and licks away the smegma, swallows them with her eyes wide open. Soon, she has a regular clientèle, all modestly content to be just fellated by the tall English chick, who will eat cock to their heart's content, but no she won't fuck. She doesn't do that, dear. She could open an art gallery with portraits of men's appendages. Soon they all taste the same and she grows used to the salty streams coursing down her throat. They like it when she swallows and some pay her more.

Some local prostitutes object to this outsider taking business away from them. They ambush her one night and kick her badly in the ribs and the face. Cut large chunks of her hair off, but she has wild curls to spare. She hurts for weeks and accepts the needle from some biker on Capitol Hill. It helps. Blanks out the hours. The memories. The guilt. The biker shares her with some friends. She needs the dope and indifferently becomes their plaything for a while. Deke, the leader, brands her, an inverted swastika on the inside of one thigh, she's property. She sleeps with three bikers in one filthy bed, they takes turns with her. The session lasts three days as they move from orifice to orifice like a sexual tag-team, violating her without feeling, playing with her like a raggedy doll, inserting objects, bottle tops, Swiss army knives, fruit. To keep her submissive they feed her the heroin. Needle marks, punctures on her arms would scare away the punters, oh yes they have plans for her, so they teach her to inject the dope into her cunt lips. The high is phenomenal.

My adventures as a whore, she reflects in a rare moment of lucidity. Might even be a book in it, she thinks. Kate in the land of cunt.

A businessman picks her up one evening while she is cruising Mercer Street. He's good to her. Convinces her not to return to the bikers. Even accepts to provide her with the now necessary junk for her habit. He sets her up in a small apartment. He's married of course. He visits her three times a week. Gives her some spare cash. She starts buying books again. But she's too passive and he soon tires of her. Takes her to a leather club and offers her in exchange for some form of life membership. She is trussed up, whipped, fucked in the darkness by one man after another until she is sore and her lower lips actually blister, she can't see any of them as a latex mask covers her face. She is roughly handled, fisted by men as well as women, tied to a rack, pissed on, slapped. In the cold morning they let her go. The businessman has taken back the keys to the flat. He's out of her life. She wanders the wet streets.

There's a reading and signing at the Elliott Bay Bookstore. It's a British mystery writer. She once met him at a party at some conference she'd had to attend in Nottingham. He doesn't actually recognise her but takes her back to his hotel afterward. She's pleased to follow, having nowhere to go. He's very full of himself, actually reads her a new story he's working on once they're in bed together. The story's ok, but the editor in her does feel it still needs some more work. He's obsessed by her arse, fondles it with genuine awe and affection, but draws back when she presents her damaged sex, and refuses to make love to her. Scared of catching something. He leaves her sleeping in the hotel room when he departs very early in the morning for his next gig in Vancouver. She has a mighty breakfast on the room. His publishers are probably picking up the tab, anyway. She smiles, the industry at least owes her this; she was bloody underpaid...

Her cunt heals. It's a resilient body part.

She finds a job in a peep show cum strip joint on the corner of First and Pike, facing Pike Place Market where they sell English papers, only a few days old. She does a girl-girl show, anonymously Frenches these other chicks while the thin audience sip their microbrews against the roar of the rock music on the sound system. One of her co-workers takes a shine to her, but Katherine easily convinces her that on stage it's fine, a job, but she has no further interest in women. The woman, her name is Judy, dolefully accepts this and they become friendly. Judy keeps on raving about the sheer beauty of Katherine's body. It's unusual, not common, she points out, you've got style, girl. She convinces Katherine to go in for a piercing. Judy sports a ring in her navel. The guys love it, you know, you'll get much better tips. Body jewellery turns them on. In the basement of a record shop that specialises in vinyl, she slips her knickers off while Judy smiles at her. The heavily-tattooed owner guides her to an operating table, lowers it and places Katherine's ankles into stirrups. He rubs ice over her cunt. Says it's better than an injection. His fingers part her and he presses against the thin hood of her clitoris, the membrane swells. Nice, he remarks. Nice and plump. As Judy, whose idea it all is explains, you'll see Katherine it's even more spectacular than the navel, hands him the sterilised needle and walks across to hold Katherine's hand. The universe explodes inside her head when he threads the needle into and straight through her clit hood. Hold on, one of them says. The pain doesn't last long. Fucking Jesus. Her lower stomach is on fire. She clenches all her vaginal muscles, breathes deep, relaxes one moment, breathes deep again, expels the air, her sphincter lets go and she feels a thin stream of shit extruding out of her back orifice. She blushes deeply. Don't worry, kid, the guy says, I'm used to it. But already the localised pain is less intense. She feels all wet around her thighs. God, has she also peed over herself? The guy wipes the black plastic table. He threads a small pearl onto the needle and it slides down to lodge itself between the fleshy hood and her bud. It's beautiful, Judy exclaims. Suits you fine says the man with the tattoos. More ice to dull the sensation. Katherine finally manages to relax. Don't touch yourself down there for a few days, the guy says as he later releases her from the table, the pearl now fixed in place, this foreign object peering out all shiny and precious from between the lips of her sex, this adornment, this jewel inside her jewel.

Judy is right. Men do like it.

A Japanese executive takes her to his suite on the top floor of the Madison-Stouffer. All Puget Sound and the islands beyond are spread out, a Cinemascope vision, beyond the bay windows. Apart from the Sky Needle, there is no way you could be any higher in all of Seattle. He strips her, places her against the tall windows, flattens her against the glass, spreads her legs, an offering to the sky outside, she has to close her eyes for fear of vertigo, only the plate glass separates her nudity from the void outside and the ground fifty or so floors down. He licks her rear, caresses the thin pale hair at the small of her back, her breasts are squashed against the glass, he slides his head in between her parted thighs, advances his tongue and inserts it from behind into her gaping cunt. He licks the pearl, chews her bud until the orgasm races through all five foot ten of her from top curls to toes. Later, he offers her an expensive jade necklace after inserting it one piece at a time into her vagina, then pulling it out with deliberate slowness, every piece bathed in her juices which he proceeds to clean with his tongue.

Her daily existence becomes a Sadeian procession of humiliation and pleasure.

One man asks her to pummel his body, harder, harder, I want it to hurt, before he can get hard. She concentrates on all those in the past, the betrayers, the abandoned, to focus her anger and strikes him with repeated fury. When the blood begins to flow from his nose and lips, she panics and flees, without payment.

She signs on for a porno loop. Three black men fuck her in the arse in quick succession while she stands bent over a wooden table. The filmmaker only has a super-8 video camera and never turns to film her face. For days afterwards, the pain endures and she hurts when walking. They've actually torn her. To think she once shuddered at the thought of Caesarians. She heals. For another pervert, she accepts to be tied up in a cave where she is administered an enema by a pocked, butch dyke, while he noisily jerks off. She wallows in the expelled liquid, rubs her skin, bathes in the shit-infested waters surrounding her on the black rubber sheet. She allows a one-legged grizzled and bitter Vietnam veteran to fuck her with his stump. While he moves the bone inside her bowels, he loudly sings *Born In The USA* off-key. And then actually cries when she leaves his motel room.

The cycle of inevitable degradation continues.

Like a penance.

One night, in dire need of junk, she's at the bar of this swank hotel, looking for passing custom when Steve Gregory walks in. Silk suit and all attitude.

'Christ, baby, you've let yourself go,' he says. 'But, you see, it's destiny, we meet again.'

She smiles feebly.

'I need cash, Steve,' Katherine says.

'You need a fix, more like. If you stay here, you're not even going to get spare change, Eddie.'

He ponders one moment.

Her brown eyes beg.

'Come to the car,' he says.

She follows.

He drives out of town. Parks in the darkness, near the Boeing fields. Slips his hand under her blouse. Feels her up.

'Still nice and firm,' Steve says. 'That's the nice thing about smallish tits, they seldom go flabby. That's an asset you've got there, honey.'

He opens the glove compartment and hands her the junk. She shoots up. It's good quality stuff. She listens to the stars out there, allows the river of ice to invade her whole body. It's too strong, like a whack to the heart, she's obliged to put her head on his shoulder.

'I'll take care of you, Eddie,' Steve says.

He doesn't even want to fuck her anymore. She's beyond it.

'See, I know this very private club down in New Orleans,' he tells her, caressing her cheeks with genuine care and concern as she dozes on. 'I think we re going to make a great team, you and me, Eddie. A great team. You'll like it there, the food is just too much and it's never cold. You've never told me if you like sea food? Do you?'

She assents with a shake of her head, his fingers move through her hair, playing with the tired curls. 'Goodbye Seattle,' she whispers. She likes it when men play with her hair. Yes, she does.

Katherine dreams.

Of New Orleans. A city she has repeatedly been told is wonderful. Fragrant. And deliciously evil.

Yet another place her lover insisted he would take her to and no, he hadn't. They had not embraced in an assortment of fancy New Orleans hotel rooms which had once been slave quarters and where cockroaches roamed free. And never would. A city of cemeteries, storms and bewitching music.

Her pale skin shivers as a last ferry leaves the harbour for the journey across Puget Sound to the scattered isles.

New Orleans.

Katherine finally sleeps. The pain goes away.

The Case Of The Locked Room Nude

It all began with a mistake.
Or a bad joke.
Someone had given Chris my name, and recommended me as a person who could help find his wife. We actually never did meet; it was all transacted over the telephone and I happily went along with the deception. He was a journalist at the BBC, specialising in business and financial matters. I knew what he looked like. Since my affair with Katherine had broken up, I'd somehow become a bit of an insomniac, waking up in the early hours of the morning when all you could watch on the box was a succession of pimply young reporters broadcasting live from the car parks of factories or some dealing room in the City, or pontificating in the studio about the coming of the information superhighway and its benefits to the business community. Business journalists? They knew as much about business as a Cambridge History graduate, and wouldn't last a fortnight in the real world of money. I suppose he was one of the worst. He'd done his pretty best to erase his northern accent but still stumbled on words like Vauxhall, Heathrow or Brighton, a wrong intonation here, a portentous tone of voice there. Anyway, he said that my name had been given to him by a contact in the arts department, a woman he'd come across on a trip to Oslo. He'd probably made a sad pass at her, and she thought it would be funny to put us together.

'They say you're the one person in London who knows most about crime,' he said.

'I suppose so,' I answered.

'Can you keep matters confidential and discreet?'

This was becoming most interesting. This guy thought I was some kind of private detective. And he wasn't just any old poor deluded guy, but actually Katherine's husband. Believe me when I tell you that when I answered his phone call, my heart began skipping the light fantastic for a moment. Had he finally stumbled on my identity?

So I nodded sympathetically, muttered a few uh-uh's over the phone, and he told me his story.

A few months back he had discovered his wife was having an affair. By then it was already over, but the thought of the four months of secret assignations, groping in hotel rooms, outright lies and her defiant and insufficiently apologetic stance afterwards had hurt him badly. Yes, he knew that one day when they were still young he had written to her that he would always stand by her and would even forgive her if she had an affair, but in practice it was different. In some colour supplement there had been an article on adultery, with a survey indicating that fifteen per cent of cuckolded husbands only would not forgive the errant partner for a one-night stand, but that nearly sixty-five per cent would not wish to continue the relationship if the affair had lasted over three months. He wanted to forgive her, to be in the minority, but it was so fucking difficult to accept; New Man, my ass!

She seemed sincere in wishing to patch things up. He had been taking her for granted, absorbed by his job and office politics at the Corporation: with the other guy it had just been lust, and lust alone. And she'd broken up with him a few days before anyway, as he was becoming too possessive. But she wouldn't reveal his identity. Someone in publishing, he guessed, as that was where she worked.

'Is that why you're contacting me?' I asked, tickled by the prospect of having to investigate myself. Just like a Philip K Dick novel…

'No, I don't think I want to know who the vile bastard is,' he answered.

Really, truly, he assured me, he had wanted to forgive her, to forget the whole sad episode, but every time he opened a newspaper, browsed through a magazine, randomly started reading a book, he was reminded of the fact that another man had touched her white skin, ruffled her curly hair, nibbled sensuously on her torn ear, licked her breasts, her sensitive nipples, spread orgasmic flush over the pale flesh of her neck and shoulders, fingered her cunt, entered her repeatedly in the missionary position and from behind, chewed on her labial folds, spent his seed inside the mad pinkness of her innards, as surely he had.

And yes, I had. A thousand times, a million times, and that wasn't all, was it? I had made love to her slowly on a rickety couch even though she was still having her period and the matted blood smeared all over my cock had seeped, jellified through the dark jungle of my pubic hair; I had coloured the pale tips of her small breasts and the lips of her sex with scarlet lipstick salvaged from her handbag, and after we had embraced it had been like streaks of blood all over my body and the crisp white sheets of the hotel room bed; I had tied her hands together with her silk scarf and attached her to the sofa legs with the belt of my black trousers; I had slapped her rump repeatedly while she rode me to the hilt, her head thrown back and sighs of tortured pleasure escaping from her lips, 'more, more' she had whispered as the pain of my palm on her skin had turned to joy; I had allowed my outstretched fingers to circle her neck and pressed gently, then harder, feeling the quickening of her pulse coursing through the vein, and she had said: 'I could let you do anything, you know, I trust you so much'; and another time: 'You're the best lover I have ever had.' Yes, I had loved her.

All this, Chris had guessed, I knew, from the look of loss in Katherine's dark brown eyes when she admitted to the affair and expressed her contrite regrets and a litany of 'Never again, never again, Jesus I swear.' But it was too late, he confessed quietly over the phone to me, the new priest in his confessional, the poison had been planted. And poison inevitably spreads. An awkward Christmas holiday divided into visits to sets of parents in Scarborough and Woking, an unreliable car which let the rain in to her irritation, the strain of seasonal jollity; later, a holiday in Tenerife where he felt awful pangs of jealousy every time a German tourist or a Spanish waiter watched over Katherine lounging in her swimsuit by the pool. This body had been shared by another. Defiled. Once, he was even physically sick.

Their rows became more frequent. It always began with a small thing. She'd forgotten to get salad or tomatoes at the Goodge Street Tesco during her lunch-break and scorned his vegetarianism in the ensuing argument. Or she'd call to say she'd be home late and he would have to prepare his own meal, she had to see an author who was coming up from Wales after office hours — an excuse she had used often when the affair was in progress. Lack of trust, jealousy. It was eating away at him.

Last week, there had been another argument and she'd walked off.

'So,' I interrupted him, 'you need me to find her, is that it?'

'Yes,' he admitted sheepishly. 'I've tried her parents, and a few girlfriends. But nobody knows where she is. I fear she's gone back to this other guy.'

I knew she hadn't. My bed was as empty as my life, and I couldn't even sleep properly for thinking of her all the bloody time, and longing like a scream for the luminous whiteness of her nudity. Often, to find the solace of dreams, I would close my eyes and jerk off silently, remembering how her long legs moved and the shape of her backside and the taste of her cunt and her heartbreaker of a smile. None of which I could tell him. Or the fact that with several women since Katherine, I couldn't even achieve suitable erections...

'Maybe she has,' I told him, thinking all the time that I hated his guts: why does a Christopher shorten his name to Chris, what a silly affectation for God's sake. I hate it when people call me Max. 'Maybe she hasn't.' And fuck you, Chris, why did she have to choose you, and who has she gone with now? I thought. 'At any rate, it's not the sort of case I can take on. Too trivial, too ordinary; come on, adultery in media circles, what could be more full of clichés? Remember, I'm the one who knows all about crime, and this sure ain't crime by a long stretch. Sorry mate, find yourself another cheap dick, try the Yellow Pages, there's a firm on Charing Cross Road.' I knew that because I'd paid these investigators to find Chris and Katherine's ex-directory number after she split, thinking maybe she'd listen to my pleading, my silly assurances of love eternal, but they couldn't even bribe a telephone company employee for the information and refunded my retainer. 'I'm sorry too,' said Chris. I put the phone down and left him with his cheap pain. Imagining briefly that soon he'd take to the bottle, sink to the gutter in the streets of the lost, just like in a novel by David Goodis.

Maybe it had started as a joke but, having betrayed both of us, where was Katherine now? Of course I had to find out; if she'd moved on to another man, I was already as much of a fool and as insanely jealous as Chris.

I sat back in the reclining black leather chair and pondered. What would Philip Marlowe do?

The evening sky outside was streaked with pink. Already spring again. My second spring without Katherine's wondrous face. I recalled our night in the Birmingham hotel. She had gone up to do a presentation to library suppliers and I'd joined her. It must have been two or three in the morning already, we'd somehow made love three times and were drenched in sweat, my cock was aching and I knew it would be on the blink until morning, and full powers again. I cuddled up to her, warmed her cold feet, and we stayed there for ages, silent, flesh pressed against flesh, and we were so close I felt like crying, wanting her more than ever. Finally I asked her, as one does, 'What are you thinking of?'

In the darkness, she answered: 'We'll be back in London tomorrow. I'll be taking that train to Charing Cross station and the office, and looking at the faces of all the people, all so sad, feeling mediocre like them. Surely there must be more to life than this.'

I didn't quite know what to say in response.

I held her even tighter against me.

'Wouldn't you just like to run away, take a train, take a plane, and just go?'

'Yeah.'

'One day, we'll go off together.'

'No, we won't.'

'Yes, we will,' I said insistently. 'Where would you go?'

'When I was younger, I often thought of pissing off to India. But it would be too hot and dirty. You can't drink the water. You mentioned how much you liked New Orleans when you went to that convention there. Yes, New Orleans. That's where I'll disappear to.'

And she fell asleep in my arms.

How the hell was I to know it was to be the last time?

My friend O'Neil had worked on the New Orleans police force. He picked me up from Moisan airport and gave me a quick tour of the Crescent City before dropping me off at my hotel in the French Quarter. He suggested we talk over a meal. I insisted we visit the Pearl just off Canal Street where the oysters are just so juicy and pungent and cheap, and by the window they have framed pages of James Lee Burke novels, in which the restaurant is mentioned. I'd always promised myself that I'd get the Pearl into a story someday, too. And the bowl of gumbo was no disappointment either.

O'Neil gave me some useful names, as I had no damn idea even where to begin my search for a tall dark-eyed blonde in this city of dreams and sudden rains.

On my first night I had a series of nightmares, a sleeping prisoner in a Cornell Woolrich story where coincidences and the implacable finger of fate kept on evoking the faces of all the women I had known and loved. I waited for Nicole by a train station clock and a policeman came to announce her death and the fact that I was a suspect. I awoke, or thought I did, and there was Lois watching me, dressed in Lisa's clothes, and when she opened her mouth, her voice was that of Marie-Jo. The clock ticked away, and I guessed that somehow my time was running out and that I had to find a woman by daybreak or my whole world would come tumbling down, or worse. But I didn't know which woman I was supposed to find. I thought of the dimple in Lois's chin, the mole on Pamela's neck, the scar on Katherine's cheek, the gap between Nicole's front teeth, the smile of Julie Christie in *Billy Liar*, Jasmine's round glasses and Julianne Moore's orange pubic thatch in *Short Cuts*. Still the minutes kept on ticking by and I was tied to the bed, Sharon Stone's opulent shape straddling me with a knife in her hand, but her face was now that of Katherine. And I missed them all, and loved them all, I wanted to shout, but no sound would come from my lips. Tick. Tock. Tick. Tock.

Struggling with my past. With images of women long gone or unattainable.

Faces. Bodies. Breasts. Legs. Lips.

Save me, please, from the memories that hurt so much.

Forgive me for the lies, the betrayals, I didn't know what I was doing.

And somewhere inside me on that endless Dauphine Street night, the voice of reason kept on saying that the damned don't die, they just have nightmares that never end.

At last, New Orleans morning and deliverance from the devils. I ventured out. Municipal workers were cleaning up Jackson Square, shovelling the deadbeats' detritus from the previous night into black plastic bags. I had a coffee at Tujague's and collected my thoughts. If Katherine had never been here before, what would she do? Well, I didn't have a clue. What a lousy private eye I was!

If she'd left their south London home in a hurry, I assumed she wouldn't have taken much in the way of reading matter. Maybe a few paperbacks at the airport. She would soon run out of things to read. I remembered the way she would cram two or three books into her bag even when we'd gone away for the weekend, although she knew there would be little time to read — we'd spend all our time fucking, talking and fucking. I knew, I was the same and never went anywhere without a few days' reading just in case, you know. We had so much in common. I phoned Réage, the cop O'Neil had recommended, and obtained a list of the town's main bookshops, both new and second-hand. As I expected, there weren't that many. New Orleans wasn't that sort of city.

I spent a couple of days describing Katherine, the way her curls flowed down over her shoulders, the sort of clothes she would usually wear, her distinctive way of walking, hunched slightly forward, how her lips curled, the irregular teeth. Surely there could not be more than one British woman answering her description in New Orleans right now, and she was bound to visit a bookshop along the way.

I was almost ready to give up when, in the last shop on my list, a dusty emporium on Chartres with a cache of book-club editions of Rex Stout and Dell Shannon mystery novels, a customer who'd heard my forlorn inquiries came over to me and said he had seen a woman answering to my description coming out of a bar on Bourbon Street the previous evening.

'I thought she did look English, you know,' the old guy said. 'But you can't be sure, can you… And that place she'd been in, not very respectable, you know. No, sir, not a place for a decent woman, you understand?'

Full moon over Bourbon Street. The drunks roll up and down the noisy arcade holding their plastic glasses of beer in precarious hands, while up there on the forged-iron balconies revellers laugh aloud at the sinners beneath and black kids tap-dance on the pavement to the rhythm of beat boxes.

Topless. Bottomless. All Nude. Male. Female. The Orgy Room. Old-time burlesque. One-dollar beer.

At the door a tall Hispanic guy urged me forward.

'Best pussy in town, sir. Come on in, entrance is free, drinks are only five bucks a go.'

I inquired after Katherine.

'Tall, blonde, small tits, biggish ass. Yeah, man, we can supply it. We sure got 'em in all colours, shapes and sizes.'

Inside.

There was a stripper dancing to a dirge of a Leonard Cohen song. Her movements were slow and languorous. She moved with deliberation across the small stage like a swimmer through water or an astronaut in space. She was a small brunette, Italian-looking, couldn't have been much over five feet tall, her dark hair was bunched in a chignon, a few strands escaping from its clutch and reaching her shoulders. She removed her spangled bra and revealed an absolutely perfect pair of breasts, delicately rounded spheres, dark areolae pointing gently upwards, firm, creamy-skinned like the rest of her body. By the bar, there was a piece of cardboard on which someone had scrawled 'Monia' in thick red felt pen. This must be her name.

A brassy barmaid served me my Coke, no ice. Five bucks, the same as beer.

The song ended.

A strong beat rushed through the club and a louder song roared its way through the industrial speakers. The Walkabouts singing Townes Van Zandt's *Snake Mountain Blues*.

Monia began to squirm to the accelerated beat, her legs dancing up and down the length of the miniature stage. She thrust her backside at some of the punters. Squatted on her haunches, projected her crotch forward, stretching the thin fabric of her G-string. Customers slipped dollar bills into the elastic holding up the small square inch of material. When she moved towards me, her body still twitching in spasms to the music, she smiled at me as she opened her legs indecently wide just a few inches away, but all I could see was the dead zone that surrounded her eyes. When I did not proffer a green bill she moved away, stood up and twirled her slight body around the central pole that anchored the stage, the smooth contours of the wood pressing between her perfect breasts and moulding her sex. The song came to an abrupt end, and Monia walked away off-stage into an area of darkness.

'That's the one thing about Noo Orleenz I don't like,' a fat Texan still wearing a ridiculous cowboy hat and sitting on my right said. 'The law don't allow them to take off their panties and show us some real pussy, like in Vegas or LA.'

A new stripper took the stage. She had a tattoo of a rose on her right shoulder and another, of a snake, circling her left wrist. I sipped my Coke, thinking who I could ask about Katherine without giving the wrong impression? Monia reappeared, wearing a silk dressing-gown over her stripping apparel. She tapped my shoulder and flashed that all-purpose smile again.

'One-to-one?' she inquired. 'There's a room at the back. I'm sure we can agree on a price.' She had a strong European accent. I nodded back. Maybe in private, she might be willing to answer my questions.

The back-room walls were plastered with movie posters. Some new, some old. *Reservoir Dogs, Choose Me, Vertigo, La Jetée.* Monia slipped the dressing-gown off. She was only wearing the thin g-string. On her own, like this, she really appeared tiny.

'Wanna fuck? Blow-job? You can come all over my tits.'

I handed her a fifty-buck note and described Katherine.

'Why didn't you say so before that you wanted the Englishwoman?' Monia said.

'Is she here?' I asked her, a tightening in my gut, a twinge of fear and expectation in my heart.

'Well, she wasn't very good at dancing, was she?' the small stripper said. 'Hernandez gave her a try-out, but she had no sense of rhythm, you know, couldn't move her butt to the beat to save her life, and she sure spooked the punters, reading at the bar all the time between sets.'

'Where is she?' I asked.

'Hernandez has got this private joint off Toulouse, very private, where they go all the way. You know, live shows. Your blonde Englishwoman, he says she's pretty good at cock-sucking, but doesn't shake enough when the men fuck her, says all she can whisper is "Jesus, Jesus" as they pound her meat, y'know, they want noise, a few screams, to make it sound real, but she can't even manage that.'

'Enough: tell me where to go.'

'Not so easy, man.'

I slipped a couple of green bills into her outstretched hand. 'Please.'

'You wait here. I'll bring her round. Hernandez doesn't like new faces at the other place.'

She moved towards the door.

'Wait,' I said. 'What if…'

'Trust me,' said Monia of the perfect breasts.

I imagine dark clouds occluding the full moon outside. The sounds of Bourbon Street reach me, quieter now, filtered through the buffer of my fear.

Katherine is in the room. Her make-up is clumsy, the gash of red over her lips isn't straight, there is a lattice of needle holes across her forearm, there are holes in her stockings.

'You?'

'Yes.'

'How did you know, how did you find me here?'

'I did. Why?'

'I had to get away. I had so badly betrayed the two of you. I hated myself. Felt guilty. Ashamed I had given in to lust and spoilt everything. Absolutely everything.'

'But this, Katherine, how could you? It's too much like a bad pulp novel. X-rated Willeford. Surely there were other alternatives?'

'Maybe. But what's the point? My heart has grown cold, so I've given myself over to lust. Perhaps I should have recognised the fact earlier, understood the nature of it. I try to forget, you, Chris, London! I take the cocks of strange men into my mouth and caress their purple crowns with the tip of my tongue and feel them grow larger and larger inside me to the point that sometimes I almost choke. None taste the way you did, though. For the right amount of cash they can fuck me, and if the money's good enough I'll take two at the same time. It doesn't make much difference, does it? And others can watch, can touch, can stretch me, tear at my orifices. It's nothing, it doesn't matter.'

'But Katherine…'

'You know, it's true what they say of black men, a lot of them here do have these huge cocks. But I can take it. The pain helps keep me awake. Look…'

She slips out of the cheap calico dress she's been wearing, unclips the garter belt and rolls down the black stockings. She's not wearing anything else.

'My skin is so very white. They like this here.'

There's a network of bruises over her thighs. Her pubic curls have been trimmed to a thin band above the lips of her bare sex.

'Is this what you remember?' she asks me.

I see the nakedness of her desire and absurdly realise that we never went dancing, and know that we shall not grow old together.

'Come,' I beckon to her. 'Let me hold you.'

I have locked the door from the inside. Her nude body moves across the purple carpet where so many others have fucked before. I open my arms: she is cold, her hair needs a wash, her curls are impossibly tangled, I recognise the particular smell of her breath as she presses her face against my shoulder. We stay like that for what feels like an eternity. Finally my fingers move to her throat, hold her firmly, then press hard against her carotid. Katherine does not resist. A nervous impulse races through her and a pale nipple quickly brushes against my elbow. I keep on pressing. She closes her eyes, keeps on leaning against me. She dies. A small trickle of urine splashes my feet as her whole body at last relaxes.

It began as a joke and ends as a locked-room mystery. Just the way I always liked my John Dickson Carr stories. Soon, Monia or someone else will knock at the door to tell me my time is up.

I unthread the belt from my trousers and attach it to a steel hook protruding from the room's ceiling. Why was it there? SM games? I find a chair which I climb on to. One end of the belt around my neck, I tighten it by a few notches.

On the floor Katherine's body lies in repose, her splendid nudity exposed for my eyes only.

When they batter the door down later, it'll be a perfect mystery.

I jump off the chair.

Co-launching the BLOODLINES crime and mystery series...

Fresh Blood
edited by Mike Ripley & Maxim Jakubowski

"Move over Agatha Christie and tell Sherlock the News!" Introducing the new generation of British mystery writers: The Do-Not Press co-launch their new Bloodlines imprint with *Fresh Blood*, the landmark anthology edited by Mike Ripley and Maxim Jakubowski.

With *Fresh Blood* there are no bodies in libraries; no amateur detectives; no neat moral solutions. There is, however: sex and violence (**Stella Duffy**, **Maxim Jakubowski**), professional criminals at work and play (**John B Spencer**, **Ian Rankin**), violence as black farce (**Graeme Gordon**), a robbery which goes badly wrong (**Mark Timlin**) and one which seems to go horribly right (**Nicholas Blincoe**), a disturbing and downbeat Inspector Resnick story (**John Harvey**) and an object lesson for young black Londoners in who not to trust (**Joe Canzius**).

To represent the work of the late **Derek Raymond**, the critic and guru of noir fiction, **John Williams**, has selected a story previously unpublished in English.

From **Denise Danks**, a sample of work-in-progress with the first chapter of a forthcoming novel and from **Chaz Brenchley**, a novella showing that, however young, the past can always catch up with you. For old time's sake, **Russell James** and **Mike Ripley** both offer the stories they wrote for the original "Fresh Blood" anthology (which never saw the light of day) five years ago.

Fresh Blood includes an introduction from each author explaining their views on crime fiction in the '90s and a comprehensive foreword on the genre from Mike Ripley.

ISBN 1 899344 03 9 — £6.99

Co-launching the BLOODLINES crime and mystery series...

Quake City
by John B Spencer

The third novel to feature Charley Case, the hard-boiled investigator of the future. But this is a future that follows the 'Big One of Ninety-Seven' — the quake that literally rips California apart and makes LA an Island. The Trent Evening Leader decreed a previous Case novel: 'The snappiest (detective story) since Farewell My Lovely... authentic Chandler style, wry and witty.'

It begins when Charley is offered a simple job...

Apartment sitting.

Simple. But before he's finished, Charley will have been embroiled in a trail of blood that leads directly to the steps of the Oval Office, and more sudden death than a popular abattoir sees in a wet Los Angeleno fortnight.

"If I hadn't had a falling out with Hetty O'Hara that last night in March at the Top Button Diner on Main Street, Santa Monica, maybe the dice wouldn't have fallen the way they did. Maybe, when Ross Helgstrom put in his call at that crazy time of eight-thirty the following morning, I'd have climbed halfway out of sweet-dream land, traced Hetty's warm contours beside me in the bed, burrowed my stubble into the soft tangle of her auburn hair, and left the phone to ring.

Maybe..."

ISBN 1 899344 02 0 — £5.99

The Users
by Brian Case

On initial publication in 1968, The Users attracted immense critical praise.

Anthony Burgess called it: 'a remarkable début — sexy without being lubricous, tough, witty, with a very palatable astringency. The dialogue is paint-fresh and the characters very much of our time'.

This brilliantly original novel offers a witty and deliciously quirky view of life in '60s Britain.

'Very, very funny. Three corpses litter the last chapters, but the wit lingers on.' — *New York Times Book Review*

The Users opens in a mortuary after a freak angling accident and sucks the reader into a deliciously bizarre story that takes in blackmail, illegal abortion, drug-addiction, student unrest, pornography, murder and the non-return of library books.

'An allegorical pop-arty, sex-thriller horror-comic... (Brian Case has) a quite uncanny skill in portrayal as well as what must be the sharpest ears in the business. A prodigious gift for dialogue.' — *The Guardian*

This re-discovered classic is available for the first time since initial publication in 1968.

'A Mills Bomb of a first novel... the whole hip glossary lurches into life.' — *The Observer*

The Users is as fresh, relevant and readable today as when it was written.

ISBN 1 899344 05 5— £5.99

Outstanding Paperback Originals from The Do-Not Press:

Funny Talk
edited by Jim Driver

A unique, informative and hilarious collection of new writing on – and around – the theme of comedy. Among the 25 authors: **Michael Palin** writes about Sid (the driver from Hell) and life on the road with the Pythons, **Jeremy Hardy** searches for links between comedy and rock 'n' roll, **Mark Lamarr** tells how a bizarre evening began with a canine death-threat, and **Hattie Hayridge** explodes a few myths about comedy, carnival time and the hazards of heckling.

Paul Whitehouse tells it how it is (roughly), **Mark Steel** reveals the problems of the Slightly Successful Comedian, **Malcolm Hardee** blows the gaff what *really* happened at Freddie Mercury's 40th Birthday Bash, **Max Bygraves** recalls buying his first car (a Ford Anglia), **Arnold Brown** recalls the roots of 'alternative comedy', and singer/songwriter **Ralph McTell** reveals a life-long passion for Laurel and Hardy.

Plus, everything you wanted to know about classic and terrible sit-coms, and entertaining and informative contributions from (amongst others) **Bob Mills**, **Bruce Dessau**, **Hank Wangford**, **John Hegley**, **Norman Lovett**, **Jon Ronson**, **Malcolm Hay**, **Alan King**, **Peter Curran**, **Anita Chaudhuri**, **Glen Colson** on his friend Viv Stanshall, comedy agent **Richard Bucknall**, and twelve new cartoons from **Ray Lowry**.

'Thoroughly excellent!' – *Time Out*.

ISBN 1 899344 01 2 — £6.95